Jared Templeton has been mated to his wolf shifter, Carson Angeni, for over a decade. Having spent the first half of his adult life as a high-paid assassin, Jared thought he'd struck a decent balance with pack life. Everything changes when their beta takes a position on the Shifter Council. That forces Alpha Declan to hold a challenge for a new Stone Ridge pack beta, which draws in unfamiliar wolves. The way one of the contestants—Larson—watches Jared arouses his suspicions, but he tells himself he's being paranoid. Jared wasn't being paranoid, and Declan's daughter Sara is kidnapped. Even though they manage to save her, Jared still blames himself and acts rashly in an attempt to catch the culprits. His choice puts not only him but Carson in a tight spot with their alpha and a few others in the pack. Will Jared remember that pack is there for each other and aren't just people to protect? Or will Jared's past catching up with him create too big a wedge to overcome?

This book is a work of fiction. Names, characters, places, and incidents either are products of the author's imagination or are used fictitiously. Any resemblance to actual events or locales or persons, living or dead, is entirely coincidental.

Checks, Balances, and Manipulation
Copyright © 2019 Charlie Richards
ISBN: 978-1-4874-2531-9
Cover art by Angela Waters

Published by eXtasy Books Inc or
Devine Destinies, an imprint of eXtasy Books Inc

Look for us online at:
www.eXtasybooks.com or www.devinedestinies.com

Checks, Balances, and Manipulation
Wolves of Stone Ridge: Book Forty-Eight

By

Charlie Richards

DEDICATION

Faith is taking the first step even when you don't see the whole staircase.

~Martin Luther King Jr.

CHAPTER ONE

Jared Templeton heard the snick of the back door, but he didn't bother to turn. He knew who it would be. The sound of Carson Angeni's voice almost made him smile — almost.

"Jared, what are you doing out here?"

Turning his head, Jared peered at his lover of over a decade. "Just enjoying the evening breeze." Knowing with Carson's wolf shifter senses — which allowed him to scent out truths, half-truths, and lies — Jared added, "And thinking."

Carson wrapped his arms around Jared. Resting his right hand on his chest, he rubbed gently over his t-shirt-clad pectorals. He slid his left hand under the hem and scraped lightly along the lines of Jared's six-pack abdominals.

Letting out a deep sigh, Jared relaxed in Carson's hold. He tipped his head, enjoying the way his lover skimmed his lips along the tendons of his neck. The hairs on his nape stood on end but in a good way.

Until meeting Carson and bonding with his wolf shifter, that had never happened to Jared before . . . and he'd certainly never allowed anyone at his back.

"What are you thinking about, love?" Carson crooned softly, his words causing warm puffs of air to tease Jared's flesh. "Something is causing all this tension in your shoulders, I'd wager."

Jared let out a deep sigh as he brought the glass he held to his lips. Searching his mind for an acceptable answer, he took a deep drink. The bittersweet chocolatey taste flowed over his tongue. As Jared swallowed the fluid, he placed the glass on the deck's railing.

"Hmm . . . that's not your usual evening beverage," Carson commented quietly, continuing to pet Jared's chest.

Chuckling softly, Jared rested the back of his head on Carson's shoulder, then turned his head. Peering at his lover out of the corner of his eyes, he teased, "Not a fan of chocolate milk?"

Carson dipped his head and captured Jared's mouth. He thrust his tongue between his lips, delving deep, mapping his mouth and caressing along his tongue. Opening happily, Jared welcomed Carson's invasion.

Just like every time Carson kissed him, Jared's blood heated and flowed south. His brain quickly began focusing on his cock. He rocked his hips backward, pleased to feel Carson's erection pushing against his ass cheeks.

When Carson lifted his head on a groan, Jared answered it with a growl.

"Yeah," Jared rumbled.

Carson's left hand eased downward. "On you, definitely tastes good," he mumbled as he flipped the button on Jared's fly, then shoved his hand inside. "Better than your usual scotch," he teased, massaging the head of Jared's swollen crown before working the sensitive bit of wrinkled flesh beneath it. "Why the switch?"

Jared hissed as he bucked in Carson's hold. "Was drinking scotch when I decided to allow the Domingo gang to know where Jerry had been taken," he admitted. "Got us in trouble."

Even as zings of blissful fire coursed through his veins and goose bumps worked through his groin, he felt a stab of self-recrimination. Jared should have known better . . . should have called in back-up. The young ex-whore was the mate of a wolf shifter, after all, even if they hadn't been bonded at the time, so he would be part of the pack . . .

family.

Family is supposed to be protected.

"I could have told you no," Carson countered as he pushed his hand deeper into Jared's pants. His thick wrist pushed the zipper down, giving him more room. Gripping Jared's dick, Carson began jacking him slowly. "Stop thinking about it."

Jared snarled low in his throat upon feeling the sweet pressure. His abdominals clenched, and his body shuddered. Desperately wanting, needing more, he reached one hand behind and between them, so he could grip Carson's crotch.

"Give me this," Jared demanded, massaging his wolf's erection through the fabric of his sweatpants. "Wanna feel you."

Even after over a decade, Jared couldn't get enough of the man behind him. He never would have thought it . . . that he would be begging to be fucked. Except, at that moment, it was what his body needed — to feel connected to his shifter.

A low, husky chuckle erupted from behind Jared, and Carson's chest vibrated at his back. His lover's hand on Jared's prick slowed. With his other hand, he lightly plucked at Jared's nipples through his shirt.

"Need my dick in your ass, handsome?" Carson rumbled huskily as he pushed harder into Jared's hold. "Want me to fill you with my seed?"

"Hell yeah, Injun," Jared instantly replied. "Pound my ass."

As Jared spoke, he released Carson's dick, which drew a soft snarl from his lover. Ignoring it, he reached into his jeans pocket and pulled out a single-use packet of lube. Holding it up, Jared wiggled it between his fingers.

"Love that you're always prepared." Carson released his nipple with one more tug, then took the packet. "My fuckin' boy scout."

Jared laughed as he shoved his pants down and bent over

the railing. "Better than a boy scout," he countered, wiggling his ass. "Assassin." Peering over his shoulder at his shifter, Jared added, "Plan for the worst. Aim for the best."

Carson shoved the front of his sweatpants down, freeing his dick.

As Carson tore open the packet, Jared took a few seconds to admire the strong lines of his smooth, hairless torso. His long, black hair flowed over his shoulders, reaching his abdominals. His thin nest of springy black curls cradling his cock was his only other hair.

Licking his lips, Jared watched as Carson squirted a little of the lube onto his long, thick, bronzed erection. Pre-cum already gleamed at the tip, and soon the rest of his flesh sparkled in the moonlight. Jared licked his lips as the pearl of translucent fluid slid down his lover's glans as Carson's big hand smoothed up and down his erection.

"Enjoying the view?" Carson's question drew Jared's attention to his partner's face.

Jared grinned as he admired the hungry expression etched on Carson's classically handsome, Native American features. "You know that I am, Injun." He wiggled his hips again. "Now put that rod of yours to good use."

Carson laughed, flashing his straight white teeth. His deep brown eyes glittered in the darkness. Using his clean hand, he swatted Jared's ass once, twice, causing delicious tingles to erupt on his flesh.

Jared growled as he gave Carson a narrow-eyed stare. "Better hurry up, or I'm gonna take matters into my own hands, Injun."

"Oh, really?" Carson smirked at him even as he gripped Jared's ass cheek and pulled it aside. As he pushed a lubed finger into his hole, his lover teased, "And how do you plan to do that?"

Carson's fingers barely there glances over his prostate as

he opened him nearly had Jared losing track of his thought processes. Rocking into his lover's touches, he relished the stretch and burn. His dick throbbed, twitching where it jutted from his groin. Jared chased Carson's fingers each time he pulled them away, and his breath caught in his throat whenever he pushed them back in.

Jared's balls began to tighten, and the base of his spine started to tingle. He was so damn tempted to reach down and grab himself. Only knowing that Carson would immediately stop what he was doing made him resist the urge. Instead, Jared held onto the railing in a tight hold.

His lover was fun like that, drawing out the blissful sparks and forcing Jared to accept what he gave him.

When Carson eased his fingers out, Jared moaned in frustration. He panted harshly as he waited . . . one heartbeat, two. Too damn long. As soon as Jared felt the kiss of Carson's cock head against his hole, he pushed out with his chute muscles and shoved with his arms.

Obviously taken by surprise, Carson stumbled backward.

Jared moved with him. He propelled them backward until his lover slammed into the side of the house ten feet behind them. Hearing Carson grunt, Jared grinned, feeling his lover's dick having sunk deep into his ass.

Reaching up, Jared grabbed Carson's neck tendons, one in each hand. He then shifted his hips forward only to push back again. Pressing Carson into the side of the house, Jared impaled himself on his lover's cock over and over.

Carson rested his hands on Jared's hips, but he didn't try to stop him. His deep moaning rumbles betrayed his enjoyment. He even spread his legs a little—probably as much as his sweatpants still around his thighs would allow. The move lowered his groin just enough to change the angle of Carson's prick, allowing him to sink even deeper every time Jared backed onto him.

It also made it so that Carson's flared crown slid over Jared's prostate with nearly every move he made.

Tightening his fingers on Carson's neck, Jared knew his short, blunt nails would be digging into his flesh. His lover growled, and Jared grinned. He knew his wolf loved to be marked by him.

"Jared," Carson muttered around another growl. "Fuck!"

Jared chuckled roughly. "Yep. That's what we're doing."

With his balls tightening and rolling in his sack, Jared sucked in a harsh breath. He was so damn close. "Touch me," he demanded, needing just a little more.

"My pleasure," Carson instantly replied. Sliding his still slightly lubed hand forward, he wrapped his fingers around Jared's throbbing erection. "Love how fucking responsive you are."

Carson pushed his other hand under Jared's shirt and squeezed his nipple.

Jared roared as his orgasm crashed through him. The zing at his nipple felt as if it transferred straight to his dick. It joined with the squeeze on his erection and the tingles from his prostate.

Continuing to rut back and forth on Carson's erection, Jared fucked himself through his orgasm. His senses reeled as he pleasured them both. He had just enough presence of mind to squeeze his chute muscles each time he popped his hips forward.

"Jared!"

Carson's roar of his name echoed in the night air. Jared hummed as he slowed his hips, reveling in the exquisite sensations floating through his body. Sighing deeply, Jared settled back against his lover, allowing the lethargy that could only be created by an amazing orgasm to settle over his senses.

Feeling Carson's lips on his neck, Jared instantly tilted his head. He felt the scrape of his wolf's sharp teeth and grinned. "You wanna bite me," Jared crooned. He loved the feel of Carson's mouth on him . . . anywhere.

In answer, Carson sank his teeth into the flesh where Jared's neck met his shoulder. The spike of pain almost instantly morphed into a bloom of heat that shot straight to his groin. His dick swelled, and his balls rolled.

Moaning Carson's name, Jared shuddered in the throes of ecstasy as a second orgasm bowled through him. Spots danced across his vision. Resting heavily against his wolf, Jared lowered his arms and reached behind him, rubbing his palms over the sides of his man's smooth, toned thighs.

"Damn, Injun," Jared mumbled as he felt Carson slide his teeth out of his flesh, then lick over the mark. He figured his smile appeared almost drunken, but he didn't care. "Somehow, you always make me feel better."

Carson nuzzled the side of his neck as he rubbed his palms under Jared's shirt. The touches were meant to soothe, to express how much his wolf cared. They did the job, too.

"Always, Jared," Carson murmured back. He pressed a kiss to Jared's neck, then softly asked, "Gonna tell me what had you so tensed up now?"

Jared inhaled deeply, then blew out the breath between slightly parted lips. He should have known his man wouldn't drop it. Nodding his head where it rested against Carson's shoulder, Jared struggled with how to explain.

"I'd struck a balance in the pack after I joined a decade ago. I had a purpose."

"Hunting the scientists," Carson commented.

Humming acknowledgment, Jared continued, "And while I don't think we've found them all, we ran out of leads after we wiped out LeReux and that dick general's network."

Carson continued to pet Jared's torso as he listened. "When we found the bongo and rabid wolf shifter."

"Right," Jared confirmed, glad the pack had eventually been able to help both traumatized shifters. "But we still haven't found the wolf shifter's brother . . . Ishmael."

"So you grew bored," Carson guessed.

"A little," Jared admitted. "And then the Shifter Council started sniffing around."

Carson nipped at Jared's neck as he mumbled, "And you had to be good."

Snorting, Jared turned his head and offered Carson an eyebrow waggle. "Oh, Injun. I'm *always* good."

Scoffing, Carson dipped his head and pressed a kiss to Jared's lips. "Not that kind of good, my mate," he stated huskily as he drew a hand out from under Jared's shirt. Carson used it to cradle Jared's jaw, urging him to tilt his head. "You've been a little reserved ever since Shane left and we held the Right for Position challenge." Dipping his head once more, Carson captured Jared's mouth in a short, primal kiss that left them both panting. "Why?"

Jared gasped, catching his breath. "I thought I was just being paranoid, but now I'm not so sure."

Carson's brows furrowed. "Paranoid? About what?"

"I didn't want to concern you if it was nothing, but after what happened with Sara, Stephani, and the gangs . . . I think someone from my past caught wind of who and where I am." Jared tipped his head and leveled a serious frown Carson's way. "I think Larson is an informant for someone, but I'm having trouble finding out who."

"Why do you think that?" Carson asked, his expression showing his concern. He lifted his hand and threaded it through Jared's short, light-brown hair. "What happened?"

"You remember when I stopped you from getting into the black SUV we rented in Los Angeles, and we took the gang's car?"

Carson nodded.

Jared heaved a sigh, then admitted, "It was because I found a bomb on it."

CHAPTER TWO

Carson moved his hands to Jared's shoulders and pushed him forward. His softened prick slipped from his lover's body, but he hardly paid any attention to that. Instead, he was too busy spinning his human mate around to face him.

"What the hell?" Carson cried, glaring at Jared. "Why the fuck would you keep a secret like that?"

Jared's hazel eyes narrowed as he scowled up at him. "For just this reason," he replied gruffly. Bending, he yanked up his pants and settled them back in place. As he did up his fly, Jared stated, "You would have overreacted, and we had shit to do there still. We had to take out the gangs first."

Lifting his hand, Carson pointed at Jared. "No more leaving me out of the loop, mate," he ordered.

Seeing the way Jared furrowed his brows and narrowed his eyes, Carson didn't give him a chance to respond. He lifted one hand and cradled his mate's jaw before slamming his lips over his lover's. Carson thrust his tongue into Jared's mouth, swirling his tongue around, taking what he wanted, and forcing his mate to submit.

Once Jared had fed Carson a moan, sagging in his arms, he eased the lip-lock to an end. He sucked in a harsh breath as he peered down at his mate. Rubbing his other hand up and down his spine, he searched Jared's face.

"Tell me you agree," Carson demanded roughly. "No more secrets."

Jared's pink and swollen lips pinched, but he nodded. "No more secrets," he agreed.

Carson jerked a nod, then eased his hold. He pecked Jared's lips once more, then released him in favor of pulling up his sweats. "Okay. So let's talk about this," he began before stepping around Jared to pick up the drink his human had left on the nearby railing. After taking a swig of the chocolate milk, Carson handed it to his lover. "First, stop reaming yourself over the coals for putting Jerry and Leo in danger. It was as much my decision as it was yours." When Jared opened his mouth, his eyes flashing with a mutinous gleam, Carson lifted his hand. "I could have said no, Jared. While you are my mate, part of that involves keeping you safe . . . not just happy. We made a mistake. We were disciplined, and now we move on. Done. Got it?"

Even as Jared grimaced, he nodded. "Got it." Rolling his eyes, he grumbled, "As if taking us off the task of tracking Larson down helps anyone."

"Raul is more than capable of getting the job done," Carson countered, wrapping his arm around Jared's shoulders and guiding him toward the back door. "You taught him every trick in the book. He'll find where Larson is squirreled away."

Jared grunted as he followed Carson's urging to head back into the home they'd shared for over a decade. Watching his mate gulp down the last of the chocolate milk as he opened the door for him, Carson just bet he was biting his tongue. His human didn't care for taking orders from another.

It was something Jared had needed to learn after integrating with the pack, and he still struggled with it.

Before Beta Shane had moved to Georgia and become a Shifter Council representative, a fairly easy truce had been drawn between everyone in the inner circle. Jared had been given plenty of leeway on how he'd been allowed to run investigations. More often than not, Jared had just told Alpha

11

Declan and Beta Shane how he was going to handle a situation.

With a new beta — Dixon Holsteen — needing strict hierarchy to establish his position, that leeway had disappeared.

Carson knew his mate chafed at the change, but he'd thought they were managing. How taking out the Robles and Domingo gangs had been handled proved he had been fooling himself. And now his alpha had told them Raul would take point on tracking down Larson — the wolf shifter who'd kidnapped two of their members and sold them to the Robles gang.

"Maybe we should take this chance to go on vacation," Carson offered, crossing to the kitchen to get himself a glass of water. "We've been busy taking care of one fire after another. How about a little R and R?"

"R and R?" Jared settled on a bar stool, wincing a little as he shifted on the padded seat.

Carson chuckled softly as he crossed to the bar's opposite side. Leaning on it, he reached out and cradled one of Jared's hands between his own. Even though he had no desire to hurt his mate, he loved that Jared could still feel him after they'd finished.

"Yeah." Carson squeezed Jared's hand. "You know. Rest and relaxation?"

Jared smirked at him, his hazel eyes twinkling. "You know, I've heard of it."

"Bet you can't remember the last time you enjoyed it, though."

His gaze smoldering, Jared countered, "I don't know. I'm pretty sure I just enjoyed some relaxation out on the deck with you just ten minutes ago." He chuckled huskily as he leaned closer. "Or are you getting old and forgot that you just had your dick in my ass?"

Carson growled low in his throat. "I remember. But that's

not a vacation."

Jared sobered, although he still smiled. Squeezing Carson's hand, he admitted, "I need to find out who placed that bomb. I had Raul disarm it and bring it back with us."

"You have an unexploded bomb in the house?" Carson growled softly. "Damn it, Jared. Where?"

Rolling his eyes, Jared straightened. "What part of disarmed did you miss?" He met Carson's gaze, holding him with their serious gleam. "Carson, I would never put you in danger like that. You know that I know how to handle explosives."

Carson winced as he realized that he'd just been questioning Jared's dedication to their bond. "Sorry, my mate." Twisting his lips into a wry smile, he admitted, "Guess I'm a little out of sorts over this whole thing, too."

Jared's smile turned understanding. Lifting their joined hands, he pressed a kiss to Carson's knuckles. His hazel eyes took on the sparkle that Carson loved so much.

"Like you said. It's done." Jared's kisses turned to nibbling as he continued to hold Carson's hand to his lips. "Now we move on and focus on something else."

Pulling his hand away, Carson took a drink of his water. Even though he'd come in Jared's ass less than twenty minutes before, he felt his blood heat at his mate's ministrations. Trying to keep his head level, Carson used the water to soothe his throat and give him a few seconds to think.

Carson knew Jared tended to use his wiles to get him to agree to shit. His mate was a master manipulator. Fortunately, Carson loved how his partner coerced him. He found it part of his human's charm.

And his challenge.

Jared was never boring, that was for certain.

However . . .

"My mate, you can't look into Larson's whereabouts, remember?" Carson warned as he returned his water to the counter before starting around it slowly. "So how do you intend to research his connection to the bomb?"

Reaching the stool, Carson gripped the seat and turned the swiveling head. "We can't go against Alpha Declan's orders. Not this time." Carson pushed Jared's legs wide and stepped between them as he offered the warning.

Jared smirked up at him. "I have no idea if it's connected to Larson or not," he countered. Resting his palms on Carson's chest, he rubbed lightly.

"Jared, you're splitting hairs."

"And if it does turn out to be attached to Larson, then I'll hand over the information to Raul," Jared continued, seeming to take Carson's warning at face value. "Plus, I'm not interested in Larson's whereabouts. You're right. Raul is damn good, and he'll take care of that. I'm interested in Larson's past. Who's paying him? Why?" After a few seconds of hesitation, Jared finished, "And if the money man is connected to any of my past hits."

Carson winced. Over the years, he'd come to grips with the fact that Jared used to work as an assassin. Sort of. His mate had a conscience . . . it was just buried way down deep and only applied to certain people—to family.

"And what happens if it is?" Carson asked curiously.

Jared hesitated, his brows furrowing. "Well, I guess that depends on who it ends up being and why."

"How will you know the why?"

Lifting a brow, Jared tipped his head to the side. His expression took on an air of speculation. "Well, I'll have to go ask him . . . or her," he added with a head bob as if just accepting that the trouble could be from a woman. Jared grinned broadly as he winked. "You did say you wanted to go on vacation, right?"

Carson groaned as he smirked at his mate. "Using my own recommendation against me, are you, my mate?"

"I just thought we could kill two birds with one stone," Jared countered with a winning smile.

Rolling his eyes, Carson allowed a low rumble to escape him. "Right."

Carson spotted the way Jared narrowed his eyes, as if he was trying to decide on another way to convince him. Threading his fingers through Jared's hair, Carson tightened his grip on the strands and urged his lover to tip his head back a bit more.

"My mate," Carson crooned, narrowing his eyes and dipping his head. He nuzzled Jared's cheek with his own, loving any opportunity to combine their scents. "If you wish to go somewhere under the guise of vacation, I will gladly accompany you."

Jared snorted. "Good save, Injun."

Carson laughed, sliding his hands down the sides of Jared's neck. Teasing along his mate's torso, he enjoyed feeling up his human, until he finally rested his palms on the tops of Jared's thighs. "Thanks." He rubbed his thumbs into the grooves where his groin met his hip. "So, where do we start?"

Chuckling, Jared lowered his hands to Carson's chest, rubbing over his abdominals. His muscles jumped at the sensual feel of his mate's touch. He felt his nipples bead, and his dick once again began to plump.

"We start," Jared began, his eyes blazing with appreciation as he began teasing his fingertips beneath the elastic waist of Carson's sweatpants. Then he grinned broadly up at him. "A shower, because I have your cum oozing out of my ass."

Barking a laugh, Carson returned Jared's smile. He released his lover's hips and took a step backward. Bending at the waist and grabbing his lover, he hefted him over his shoulder as he straightened.

Carson strode through their home, heading toward their bedroom and the massive attached ensuite. He had every intention of making certain his lover was squeaky clean.

Then I just might dirty him up all over again.

The ring of the doorbell pulled Carson out of his sleep. Lifting his head, he turned and peered at the alarm clock sitting on the nightstand. Carson heard the doorbell again—rung several times in succession—and realized who it was that was dropping by before eight AM on a Saturday morning.

Carson rolled out of bed and crossed to his dresser. Opening the drawer, he snagged a clean pair of sweatpants.

"God, what is she doing here so early?" Jared grumbled.

The creak of the bed told Carson that his lover was also rising. He opened the drawer to the left of the one he'd just closed and grabbed a pair of sweats for Jared. After turning and tossing them to his mate, Carson pulled on his own pants.

By the time Carson reached the front door, the bell was ringing again. He opened it, ready to growl. Except, when he spotted the expression on Sara's face, Carson spread his arms, instead.

Sara choked out a gasp as she crossed the threshold and stepped into Carson's arms.

Carson tucked Sara's slender frame against his own, wrapping her in a tight hug. Rubbing one palm up and down her back, he took a step backward, drawing Declan's daughter with him. With his free hand, Carson reached past her and shut the door.

To Carson's surprise, the noises he heard Sara making weren't the sound of tears. Instead, she was growling. Her scent also betrayed her feelings—indignant rage.

Resting his free hand on Sara's nape, Carson squeezed lightly, urging her to look up at him. "Talk to me," he murmured, trying to sound encouraging. "What has you so worked up?"

Sara heaved a sigh, her brown eyes shining with frustration. "I wanna kill him," she snarled, continuing to growl under her breath. Then she rolled her eyes and shook her head. "I love him already, but I still wanna kill him! Does that make sense?"

"Definitely," Carson assured. After pressing a kiss to the slender brunette's forehead, he eased his hold and turned her. "He's your mate. Just because you meet doesn't mean building a relationship will be all roses and sunshine." As Carson started them both walking through the house toward the dining room, he scoffed softly, "Hell, you were around when I met Jared. And I know you were young, but remember when Lark and Declan first got together?"

Heaving a sigh, Sara muttered, "Yeah, yeah. Dad says the same thing. A relationship takes work."

Carson knew she meant Lark. Sara referred to Declan as Father.

"It also takes two to make it work," Jared commented from where he stood pouring coffee into mugs. With sleep-tussled hair, he smirked in their direction. "What did the asshole do this time, Sara?"

Sara McIntire, adopted daughter of Alpha Declan McIntire and his mate Doctor Lark Trystan, pulled away from Carson and plopped onto a chair. She gratefully accepted the cup of coffee Jared provided—heavy on the sugar with just a dash of half and half. After taking a sip and humming appreciatively, she set the mug in front of her on the table before shoving her fingers through her thick dark-brown hair, pulling the hair tie out in the process.

As Sara retied her hair into a messy bun, Carson knew she was stalling. After receiving a morning kiss as well as a cup of coffee from Jared, he settled on a chair beside her. Jared eased onto a chair on the other side of Sara.

"Well?" Carson pressed, touching the back of her hand with his fingertips. "It's not even eight in the morning. What could have possibly gone wrong so early?"

Carson knew that, while in Los Angeles being rescued, Sara had realized one of her rescuers was her mate. The detective by the name of Ricky Malone had already known about paranormals, and his assistance had been recommended by a nomadic shifter gang the Stone Ridge wolf pack considered friends. Too bad Ricky wasn't more understanding with his knowledge.

Ricky didn't think much of paranormals' propensity for taking matters into their own hands. He'd helped them because his brother was mated to a shifter . . . oh, and because he'd made a promise. Evidently, that was the human detective's one redeeming quality—in Carson's eyes anyway—Ricky always kept a promise, no matter how difficult.

Too bad he's more than a little bit of an asshole.

Due to the fact that Sara recognized Ricky as her mate—the one and only person on the earth that she could form a soul bond with, connecting their life threads—Declan had made the decision to bring Ricky back with them, moving the belligerent detective into their home. Carson wasn't certain that had been the right decision, but he didn't make it a habit of questioning his alpha. If it had been up to him, he would have set up an apartment for Sara there and figured out a way for them to run into each other over and over—giving the mate-bond time to do its work.

Sara explained how she'd run into Ricky in the kitchen that morning, and when she'd asked him if she could make him anything, the detective hadn't given her the time of day. Instead, he'd ignored her and returned to his room.

Carson wondered how he could help get Ricky's head out of his ass.

CHAPTER THREE

Sara once again tugged her hair out of the bun on the top of her head. Scrubbing her fingers through her hair, she scratched at her scalp. The massage not only helped ease her stress, but it gave her something to focus on other than that blasted human.

My mate. The asshole.

That was what Jared called him. Unfortunately, he was right. The old saying *it takes one to know one* totally applied to Jared and Ricky.

Living at the alpha house, having been adopted by Alpha Declan, Sara knew just about everything that went on in the pack. She also kept her mouth shut about it. Jared Templeton was sort of an antagonistic dick with his sharp wit, cutting tongue, and dark, dry humor. His wolf shifter mate, Head Enforcer Carson Angeni, was a strict, down-to-earth and follow the alpha anywhere type of man.

They were opposites.

Yet, somehow . . . they worked.

On top of that, Sara liked them. They'd always been nothing but kind to her over the years. Of course, some might not consider it kind that Jared had helped her set up some secret porn subscriptions because Alpha Declan was so dominant that she couldn't date . . . but in Sara's mind, that just made him seem like the perfect uncle.

Knowing all that, Sara had decided to come to them when she knew she was losing her temper. As a gazelle shifter, she didn't really have much of one, but every once in a while . . .

and this was one of those times. The fact that she was horny as hell and more than a little hurt probably didn't help matters.

"So, how do I get him to talk to me?" Sara asked absently. A fresh stab of sadness sank into her heart. Rubbing her thumb over the rim of her coffee mug absently, Sara commented, "I mean, I say good morning, and I get a mumble. I ask him if he wants breakfast, and he walks back upstairs." Groaning, Sara glared at her toffee-colored drink. "He's so rude, and yet, I still want to rub my hands over his broad shoulders and skim my fingers over his five o'clock shadow, and I want to peel off those skin-tight t-shirts he wears and—"

Jared snorted, chortling. "We get it, honey." He patted her hand, his eyes twinkling with mirth. "You want to strip him down and ride him like a pogo stick."

Sara winced as her face heated. She just knew she was blushing, but she couldn't help it. She couldn't believe she'd just blurted all that out.

"Relax," Carson rumbled, leaning over and squeezing her shoulder. "We get it. We really do."

Nodding, Sara heaved a sigh. She flashed a grateful smile between the men, then lifted her sweetened coffee to her lips. After taking a sip and lowering it back to the table, Sara glanced between them again.

"So, um. Any ideas?" Sara sure hoped they knew some way to help get the stick out of Ricky's ass.

"Gotta get him to talk to you, first," Jared mused. Tipping his head, he stared at the ceiling. His eyes narrowed to slits for a few seconds before he turned and gave Sara a cheeky smile. "I don't suppose you'll allow us to tie him to your bed." Jared waggled his brows. "I'm sure he'd talk to you then."

Sara barked a laugh even as her cheeks heated once more.

"Um . . . wouldn't that start a lot of yelling, though? Probably not a good idea."

Even as Sara denied the idea, thoughts of what Ricky would look like tied to her bed flooded her mind. Her heart fluttered in her chest as she imagined his strong arms spread, ropes binding his wrists to the thick posts of her bed frame. He would be naked, leaving a thick coat of chest hair on display. The strands would taper to a treasure trail that would lead to his long thick cock, which would jut from his groin, eager for her touch.

Swallowing the moisture in her mouth, Sara felt her blood pool lower, making her body throb with need.

"So . . . you do like the idea." Carson's deep voice cut into Sara's thoughts.

Blinking once, twice, Sara recalled where she was and who with. She forced herself to meet Carson's mirth-filled dark eyes. "Um, I-I could see the benefits to it," she muttered, shifting with her sudden discomfort.

Carson patted her wrist before scowling at a still-smirking Jared. "Control yourself, my mate."

"If you insist, Injun," Jared quipped back in a way that had Sara thinking he didn't really intend to obey, but Carson didn't say anything about it.

Sara cleared her throat. Even though she felt reasonably amused at Jared's antics, she forced a scowl to her lips. "No tying up my mate," Sara stated firmly. Straightening in her seat, she added primly, "If anyone is going to tie up Ricky, it's me."

Just that acknowledgment caused a flutter in Sara's chest.

Jared's lips curved. "We could find out if Ricky likes bondage." Giving her an assessing look, he added, "You are a shifter, after all. It would be easy for you to overpower him."

"Oh, for goodness sake," Sara cried. "No more talk about

helping me tie up my mate." Rubbing her hands over her arms, she grumbled, "It's making me even more horny, and I can't do anything about it."

Carson's brows shot up as he nodded. "Right. Sorry." Curving his lips into a twisted smile, he added, "Believe it or not, I do know how that feels." Then Carson cleared his throat and stated, "Time for a phone call. Let me go get my cell."

Sara watched as the big Native American rose and headed toward the hallway that Sara knew led to the master suite.

Jared also rose. "Why don't you make yourself at home, Sara. I'm going to brush and piss and make certain Carson does the same." Shrugging unrepentantly at his bluntness, he added, "You pulled us out of bed, after all."

Sara glanced over at the oven clock and winced. She'd always been an early riser. "Right. Sorry." Rising from her chair, too, she urged, "Take your time. I'll make you guys breakfast." She spotted Jared's lifted brow and told him, "It's the least I can do for barging in on you on a Saturday morning."

Nodding, Jared turned away while giving her a thumbs up.

Figuring that was permission, Sara downed the rest of her coffee, then moseyed into the kitchen. She hummed under her breath as she made herself a fresh cup. Then Sara began opening cupboards and pulling out stuff.

Ricky leaned against the window sill and stared out the window. With his arms crossed over his chest, he grumbled under his breath as he did his best to ignore his throbbing dick. He clenched his teeth and tried to focus on the view outside.

There was a massive back deck complete with a large,

built-in stone grilling monstrosity. A huge yard sprawled beyond that until it hit a tree line of pines. The woods covered the expansive mountains he could see in the distance.

I bet Sara likes running in those trees.

Ricky winced at the thought, but he couldn't stop the next one.

What does she look like as a wolf?

Having seen ex-fellow-detective Draven Mansetti's lover and partner—Vail Tamang—change into a wolf, Ricky understood the concept. He knew the process sounded painful and grotesque, but they'd described it to him as a really good stretch after sitting for too long. The man's animal had been large with dark-brown fur and quite handsome in its own way.

Ricky wondered if the shifter's different sizes, as well as sex, would make a difference. He bet Sara would be so much prettier. Uncrossing his arms, he reached down and adjusted his hard dick even as he rolled his eyes.

"Good grief." Ricky turned and flopped onto the bed. "What the fuck is wrong with me?"

Even as Ricky grumbled the words, he unbuttoned and unzipped his fly. His underwear-covered erection immediately burst from between the flaps. Lifting his hips, Ricky pushed his pants and boxer-briefs halfway down his thighs.

Wrapping his right hand around his shaft, Ricky cupped his balls with his left. He rolled his testicles in his sack as he began stroking his prick. His cock throbbed, and he knew from experience that it wouldn't take long.

Ricky knew it would be blamed on the mate-pull thing that the paranormals talked about, but that didn't make it any easier to control. Any time he was in the same room as Sara, his blood heated and flowed south. He would gain a rock-hard erection faster than he thought could be possible.

It didn't even matter if he took a cold shower. He couldn't get rid of his boner until he gave in and rubbed one out.

Unfortunately, that would only last until he saw Sara again . . . or heard her voice . . . or even just thought about her.

Even as guilt filled Ricky—he felt as if he was robbing the damn cradle—he allowed his thoughts to turn to her. Recalling how, that morning in the kitchen, her hair had been tied in a messy bun at the top of her head, he'd longed to pull the hair bobber out. He wanted to see her long, thick tresses tumble down and spread across his chest. Ricky just bet the smooth locks would feel fantastic sliding around his erection—the silky strands teasing the sensitive skin of his shaft.

Those thoughts were immediately replaced by the images of Sara opening her sweet red lips and wrapping them around the head of his shaft. The suction would feel so damn fantastic. Ricky had seen the lust in her eyes, and he imagined that, as she sucked him, she would look at him just like that . . . as if pleasuring him was her favorite activity on the planet.

She's a shifter. It will be.

Fuck!

Ricky sucked in a harsh gasp as the idea of enjoying Sara's sweet, sensual body any time he wished crashed through him . . . bringing with it his orgasm. His balls pulled away from his palm, tightening pleasantly. He felt the throb intensify in his cock as his seed spilled across his abdomen in sharp, bliss-inducing spurts.

Panting softly, Ricky reveled in the waves of euphoria caused by his release. His senses floated, and he hummed softly. Ricky released his genitals, flopping his hands to the sides of his hips, and just . . . enjoyed.

As Ricky lay there staring at the ceiling, another thought pushed into his mind.

When was the last time I found someone that turned me on like this?

Just as quickly, Ricky knew the answer.

Never.

It's a shifter thing, then, right?

Yep. So what?

It's not real.

Sure it is. Why wouldn't it be considered real?

"Oh for the love of Christ," Ricky grumbled, flopping his hand toward the nightstand. He grabbed the box of tissues and began cleaning himself up. "Now I'm arguing with myself. This just keeps getting better and better."

Ricky had just finished dropping the soiled tissues into the waste bin beside his bed when the trill of his phone caught his attention. Reaching over, he lifted a brow when he saw the name. He hadn't heard from his ex-coworker in . . . several years.

Although, Ricky could guess why he was hearing from him now.

Accepting the call, Ricky greeted, "Draven. I have a funny feeling I know why you're calling."

"In many areas of life, you are an extremely perceptive man, Ricky," Draven Mansetti greeted back. His warm tenor flowed in Ricky's ear as soothing as it had ever been. A hint of amusement filled his tone as he continued, "You found your mate. Why are you fighting your bond? You're only making you and Sara miserable, and I can guarantee that after you give in, you'll kick yourself for wasting even a minute where you could have been together."

Ricky rolled his eyes.

And now I remember why I haven't missed him all that much.

Heaving a sigh, Ricky grumbled, "This thing between us isn't real, Draven." He voiced his earlier concern. "It's a manipulation of hormones and pheromones."

To Ricky's annoyance, Draven laughed. "Oh, Ricky. All attraction is a manipulation of hormones and pheromones. Why is this any different?" Draven didn't give Ricky a chance to reply. "Just because you feel attraction to a shifter, don't discount it."

Ricky flopped back on the bed and once again stared at the ceiling. "Sara's nineteen. Did you know that?"

"So."

Groaning at Draven's response, Ricky pointed out, "I'm forty-one years old, Draven. That's over a twenty year age difference." He heaved a put-upon sigh before mumbling, "I'm twice her age. Robbing the fucking cradle."

"Ah, is that what truly troubles you?" Draven's curious tone filled the line. "Or is it just another excuse?"

"It's not an excuse, Draven," Ricky barked gruffly. Just discussing the gorgeous brunette was once again causing his dick to plump. "It's the truth. How would it ever work? How can we possibly have anything in common?"

"Have you taken the time to talk to her at all?"

Ricky gritted his teeth. "Talking to her is . . . difficult."

"Because it makes your dick stand up and beg for attention?"

Growling, Ricky did his best to ignore the embarrassed heat creeping up his neck. He'd never been one to discuss his liaisons. It just wasn't his way.

"Look. Ricky." Draven heaved a soft sigh, then murmured, "You're a semi-vegetarian . . . so is she. Why don't you start there?"

Ricky couldn't help the surprise flooding him. "How is a wolf shifter a semi-vegetarian?"

Draven chuckled. "You really need to start talking to her, Ricky." His amusement came through loud and clear. "Sara isn't a wolf shifter. She's a gazelle shifter."

"A g-gazelle?" Disbelief flooded Ricky. "No fucking way. Her father's the alpha of a wolf shifter pack."

"Sara is adopted."

Huh. Could that be a starting point?

"Yeah, but what about the age difference?" Ricky pointed

out. "She's so young. How can she possibly know that I'm the one she's gonna want in ten years . . . or five years . . . or hell, next year?"

"Did you forget that paranormals who bond with their fated mate, they mate for life?" Draven heaved a sigh. "Ricky, Sara will never want another . . . ever. That's the way of paranormals. You know this."

Ricky did know.

But still.

Groaning, Ricky knew he was repeating himself, but it just had to be said. "She's nineteen!"

"Tell me this, Ricky. When Sara is two hundred and nineteen and you are two hundred and forty-one, is that twenty-two year gap really going to make that big of a difference?"

Ricky sucked in a harsh breath. "Holy shit!"

I completely forgot all about that.

CHAPTER FOUR

Leaning over the bomb resting on his worktable, Jared carefully cataloged every last bit of it. He grumbled under his breath as he searched for any hint of something that could give away the creator. Most bomb makers had a signature . . . something that tied them to every piece they'd ever made.

A grunt of pleasure escaped Jared. "Gotcha," he whispered. Then he frowned as he realized the implications. "You only work for three people, Castrose. And I've never had dealings with any of them." Cocking his head, Jared muttered, "So what's going on?"

The sound of Carson walking down the stairs to his basement work area drew Jared's attention. Turning his head, he watched his lover enter the room. After accepting a kiss, Jared indicated the seat next to the wall.

"What'd you find?" Carson asked as he drew a chair up to the table and sat down.

"Nothing good, I'm afraid," Jared admitted. He pointed toward a tiny, complicated coupling between a series of wires. "See the way this is twisted in that intricate knot?"

Carson leaned close, moving a wire out of the way, then nodded. "I do."

"Unless we have a copy-cat, that indicates the bomb was made by a guy named Castrose Zukan. He learned his trade in the Swedish military, but as soon as he *retired*" — Jared lifted his fingers and made air quotes — "he disappeared. Castrose's bombs began appearing in private residences of the rich and famous, the homes of drug kingpins, and even the occasional government building."

"Was Castrose tracked down?" Carson narrowed his eyes as he focused on Jared. "Is he someone we can go talk to?"

Jared eased back in his chair and crossed his arms over his chest. "Plenty of people have tried to find him, but whatever his connections are, someone wants him alive." Holding his lover's gaze, he explained, "Every time someone drew close to finding him, all they walked in on was an empty house stripped of anything that could possibly point at where he went."

"So he's a ghost."

Nodding, Jared repeated, "Yep. He's a ghost."

Carson heaved a deep sigh as he rubbed his palm over his high-cheek-boned jaw. "So what do we do?"

Jared waggled his brows at Carson. "Just because Castrose is a ghost doesn't mean he can't be found."

"Think much of yourself, don't you?"

Grinning, Jared laughed softly. He knew his lover didn't mean anything cutting by his words. His man knew he had a big ego and an even bigger propensity to prove it was well deserved.

"Not just me," Jared countered. With a snort, he rolled his eyes. "While it's true Castrose has never had me looking for him"—he focused a smug grin Carson's way—"but those who've always tried to track him down have been human. Human agencies, governments, gangs, and the like."

Carson leaned over and grabbed Jared's neck and tugged. Jared went with the move, accepting his lover's lips against his own. He opened instantly, enjoying his wolf shifter's masculine flavor and dominating tongue.

When Carson broke the kiss, he put a few inches between their faces and murmured, "My mate you may be, and you have increased strength and agility because of it, but you're still human."

Jared grinned broadly as he leaned forward and pecked a kiss to Carson's mouth. After a gentle nip and suckle to his man's lower lip, he drew away again. He peered into Carson's deep brown eyes, enjoying the look of arousal he saw swimming within their depths.

As much fun as it would be to act on the desire Jared saw there, they had other matters to deal with first.

Too damn bad.

His dick twitched, but he ignored it.

"Yes, I am human, but I think I've proven over the years just how damn good I am at finding things." Grinning broadly, Jared lowered his voice to a husky rumble as he added, "Besides, I have help from the paranormal. Since we called Draven, and the vampire-warlock has agreed to come here to help knock some sense into Ricky's head, perhaps he can cast a spell or two for us." Straightening, Jared told him, "It would help save lives, after all."

"My silver-tongued devil," Carson murmured before claiming Jared's lips again.

Carson eventually broke the kiss, only to smirk at Jared. "So, you intend to use magick to find this guy?"

Jared shrugged. "Sure. Why not?"

"Okay." Carson nodded. "So once you find this guy, what do you intend to ask him?"

"Simple." Jared shrugged. "I'm gonna ask him how one of his bombs ended up under our SUV, and if he lies, you're gonna tell me." Growling softly, Jared finished, "And if he continues to lie, we'll *convince* him of why telling us the truth is in his best interest."

"And then what?"

Jared held Carson's gaze as he shrugged. "We find out why whoever that person is is trying to kill me . . . or you. Then we stop them."

Carson hummed as he nodded. "Sounds good."

Straightening in his chair, Jared grabbed his cell phone from the table. He quickly dialed a number, then put the phone on speaker and placed it back on the table. He listened as the line rang. After the third ring, Jared worried he was going to have to leave a message.

Jared scowled, a surge of impatience filling him.

He really didn't want to have to leave a message.

"Suns and stars. I just got off the phone with Ricky an hour ago." There was a clear note of exasperation in Draven's tone as it came through the line. "What could the bonehead have possibly done already?"

Jared chuckled as dry amusement quickly replaced the impatience. "Nothing that I know of. Sara took a run to cool off, so I doubt she's with him." After a glance at a smirking Carson, Jared quickly added, "I have another reason for calling."

"Oh? What's that?" Draven asked, curiosity coloring his words.

Opening his mouth, Jared hesitated.

Is it bad form to ask about magick over the phone?

Jared was human, so until then, the thought hadn't occurred to him. Drawing his brows into a scowl, he leaned closer to his lover and muttered, "Are there rules about talking about Draven's abilities on an open line?"

Carson lifted his hand and waggled his hand in a *sort of* motion.

Nodding, Jared asked, "Is your line secure?"

"I'm using the *Bluetooth* in my motorcycle helmet as I drive down the highway, so you decide," Draven answered. "Anything can be hacked, I suppose."

"Hmm." Jared hesitated, then he shrugged. "Well, if you can't answer something, feel free to just say so."

Draven snorted. "I always do."

Jared grinned and leaned on the table. He found Draven's attitude refreshing. "Very well. If I give you a name, do you

31

have the ability to locate someone?"

"Species?"

Lifting his brows, Jared couldn't help but ask, "It matters?"

"It does."

Huh. I'll have to ask him for more on that another time.

"Human," Jared told the paranormal.

"If you have something of his . . . or hers," Draven told him. "An article of clothing recently worn. Something that they would have been in contact with a lot . . . and recently."

Jared's gaze strayed to the bomb as he nodded absently. "Well, I have something he would have spent a lot of time working on, but I don't know how long it's been out of his possession."

"Okay. I can give it a try," Draven told him.

"I appreciate that." Jared reached for the phone, preparing to end the call.

"Who are you looking for and why?" Draven asked curiously. "And why can't you just look him up the usual way?"

Jared relaxed back in his chair and stretched his arms over his head. "I have a bomb sitting in my workroom, and I want to find the guy who made it."

Through the line came the sound of a muttered curse and the squeal of brakes.

A second later, Draven's voice became louder once again. "Damn it, Jared. A little more tact, next time, huh? You nearly made me wreck my bike."

Rolling his eyes, Jared snorted.

"Good thing you have those amazing reflexes, then, huh?" Carson stated, his tone dry.

"And you asked," Jared pointed out.

"Yeah, I did," Draven replied on a sigh.

Jared figured he could explain the rest later. "What's your ETA?" he asked, wondering when the biker would arrive.

Draven hummed for a few seconds. "Looks like we'll be

there day after tomorrow. Around noon, give or take."

"We?" Jared reached out and threaded his fingers with Carson's. The impulse to touch the sexy wolf shifter any time he was near always seemed to surprise Jared, but he had no interest in fighting it. "Who all decided to join you?"

Knowing Kontra Belikov considered a couple of dozen men under his care, Jared wondered who would be joining Draven—besides his wolf shifter mate, Vail, of course.

"This is our first big run this spring," Draven told him. "So just about everyone who could." The vampire-warlock's chuckle came through the line. "I imagine we booked just about every room in Stone Ridge."

With a soft laugh, Jared replied, "Your gang is good for business."

As he spoke, his focus strayed back to Carson. A groan rumbled from his throat, and his heart rate spiked. He swallowed hard as moisture pooled in his mouth.

Jared's voice was husky when he muttered, "I gotta go. Talk to you later."

Without waiting, although he did hear a chuckle sounding from his phone's speaker, Jared reached out and disconnected the call.

Turning his attention back to Carson, Jared admired the pretty view. Since his lover rarely wore a shirt around their home, his broad torso was on clear display. The gorgeous part was how, at some point during the call, Carson had shoved down the front of his sweatpants and pulled out his cock and balls. His legs were splayed, and his bronze, swollen shaft jutted from the thin nest of curls.

Carson still held Jared's hand, but with his other, he was busy fondling his testicles.

Sucking in a harsh breath, Jared admired his lover's masculine beauty. "I—"

"I really thought it would be harder to track you down,

Coleson."

Jared snapped his gaze away from his lover's erect dick and peered toward the speaker who was standing halfway down the stairs behind him.

What the fuck?

His heart tripped in his chest for a whole new reason.

Taking in the shaggy, black-haired man standing with one foot cocked up and resting on the stair above where he stood, Jared felt a trickle of sweat drip down his back. The stranger had aristocratic features, except for the bump in his nose that betrayed it had been broken. His full lips were curved into a mocking sneer.

It was the gun he held in his hand, however, that concerned Jared the most.

Oh, and just how the hell did he get in here?

Jared lifted a brow as he straightened in his seat, releasing Carson's hand. Out of the corner of his eye, he spotted Carson's indecision . . . and the wilting of his cock.

Too bad.

From Carson's expression, Jared knew what his lover was silently wondering.

Do I shove the pants off and shift? Or do I put it away and fight like a human?

Jared was happy to leave that up to his wolf, because one way or another, the stranger wouldn't be allowed to leave.

"It's really not very nice to barge into other people's homes," Jared commented mildly as he turned in his seat as if attempting to get a better view of the man. He used the move to cover the way he reached under the table with his left hand.

With a derisive snort, the man replied, "As if you have any room to talk, assassin." His grin widened. "You know, there's a pretty impressive reward for your head. I'm lucky I found you first" — his eyes narrowed as his lips curved into a cold sneer — "Jared Templeton. That *is* your real name, isn't

34

it?"

It took every bit of self-control Jared contained to keep from whipping the gun out and just shooting the bastard.

"You are indeed good," Jared applauded the man. "I've never had anyone track me down before." Lifting one brow, he asked, "What's the reward on me? And who's paying?"

"Now that I know your real name, I've discovered three hits out on you by different organizations," the man told him, smirking. "The Aurora's are offering fifty grand for Therion. The Mohamed's are offering a hundred grand for Domingo." While waggling his brows, he stated, "But I think I'll take your head to the Sanchez cartel, seeing as they're offering a million for Coleson."

Chatty and cocky. Dumb ass.

"A million," Jared mused. "Damn." Shrugging his shoulders, he commented, "That is an impressive amount."

"Yep." The stranger indicated with his gun. "Stand up. Hands over your head."

"You really should have had us raise our hands before," Jared commented. Even as he spoke the words, he rose, twisted, and whipped his left hand around.

Good thing I'm ambidextrous.

The report of his pistol reverberated within the walls of the basement, making Jared's ears ring. The fact that more shots began to boom through the room didn't help. He ignored it even as he dove to the right, rolled once, then finished in a crouch that allowed him a better view of the stairs. Pinning his gaze on the stranger, he aimed at the stumbling man and fired again.

Carson leaped over the railing, easily landing a couple of stairs above the guy as he slid down them on his backside.

Jared watched as his mate grabbed the gunman's wrist and squeezed. A scream filled the air as he dropped his weapon. The man's shock couldn't have been more evident as he attempted to yank away from Carson.

Upon rising, Jared strode over to the fallen man. He used a foot to push the dropped gun halfway across the room and well out of the man's reach. Then he pointed his own weapon at the bleeding man's knee.

"Now, let's try to chat like civilized people, hmm?" Jared gave the man a wicked grin as he watched Carson release the stranger and sit down on the step two above where the guy had slid to the bottom of them. "How did you get into my house without tripping an alarm?"

CHAPTER FIVE

"Uh, I actually think that was my fault," Carson admitted, rubbing at his jaw. "I didn't reset it after Sara left."

Carson would be the first to admit that he did that a lot. Having lived in the mountains for so long, he often left them unlocked when he was home. As a dominant wolf shifter, he rarely worried about his safety.

Now I will, though . . .

Jared hummed as he flicked a narrow-eyed glance Carson's way.

"Sorry, love," Carson murmured, feeling the urge to apologize.

Shrugging, Jared winked at him. "No harm done." Then he smirked at their uninvited guest. "To us, anyway." Tapping his forefinger on the side of his gun, Jared grinned at the guy. "Next question. How did you discover my real identity?"

Carson really wanted to know that, too. His lover guarded his information jealously.

To his annoyance, the man stated, "You give me medical attention, and I'll tell you."

Jared snorted as he shook his head. Then he pulled the trigger.

Grimacing, Carson didn't know what was worse — the ringing of his ears from the shot or the human's scream of agony. He took in the mess Jared had just made of the guy's leg and winced.

Okay. That's worse.

"You're not getting out of here alive, man," Jared stated bluntly. "But how you go out depends on you." His expression darkened as he moved his hand so the gun was pointing at the man's other leg. "I'm happy to give you a nice quick death. A bullet to the head. But before I do, I need to know what you know, so start talking. How did you find me?"

Carson cleared his throat, gaining Jared's attention. "You ever hear that expression *you catch more flies with honey*?" As he spoke, he couldn't help the teasing in his tone.

Jared smirked. "I only have a limited supply of honey, Injun." He waggled his brows as he added, "And it's reserved for you and family." As Carson watched, the blood appeared to drain from Jared's face. He snapped his attention back to the gunman. "Have you touched my family?" His voice turned into a low snarl, and he pressed the thumb of his right hand into the wound situated high up on the man's right shoulder. "Have you told anyone?"

"Okay, okay!" the stranger whined, cringing away from Jared's touch. "Come on, man. You're in the business. You know how it is."

"I *was* in the business," Jared countered, frowning at the guy. "I've been out for over a decade. Now tell me what I want to know."

"There's one other guy who's probably close to figuring it out. I know him only as Scottson, but I'm better with a computer," the man claimed. "You left a money trail when you turned down the Danner job fifteen years ago."

"Danner job," Jared whispered, his eyes narrowing. Then he rolled his eyes. "Oh, for the love of—" Jared growled. "That fucker's family didn't know how to do anything right. That's one of the reasons why I—" Once again, he cut himself off.

Then Jared glared at the man bleeding all over the basement floor and last couple of steps. "And my family?"

While Jared and Carson didn't associate with them much, he knew that his mate's parents lived about forty-five minutes away in Colin City. His two sisters did, too. His older sister, Brandy, was married and had two young children. His younger sister, Patricia, was still single, although Carson didn't think that would be for much longer. She'd been dating the same guy for nearly a year, and it appeared to be pretty serious.

"No, Coleson," the gunman replied, his voice beginning to weaken. "They're not part of the hit."

"Jared?" Carson used the one word as a warning.

Heaving a sigh, Jared nodded. "Grab the first aid kit and shit to wrap his wounds while I call the alpha-mate."

Carson's brows shot up. "You're gonna try to save him?" He hadn't expected that. In fact, Carson had thought he would have followed through on his word and taken him out, ending his suffering.

"He was just doing a job," Jared pointed out as he whipped his shirt over his head and wrapped it around the man's ruined knee. As he worked, Jared shrugged, adding, "Besides. I have a few more questions to ask him and won't get the answers if he dies on me."

Accepting that, Carson rose and bounded up the stairs. He quickly located not only the first aid kit, but he grabbed hot water and clean towels. When he returned to the basement stairs, Carson noticed Jared on the phone—the device tucked between his shoulder and ear—even as he wrapped strips of what was once his t-shirt around the man's knee.

Carson rested the bowl of water on the step, then crouched beside the man. He opened the first aid kit as he asked, "That shot you put through his left side, is it a through and through like his shoulder?"

Jared nodded even as he continued to give a report to

someone on the phone. From his words of how he shared that an attack had happened in his home and how he encouraged to have words of caution spread amidst the pack, Carson bet he was talking to their alpha. It wasn't until Jared received a response that he realized he was wrong.

"I'll begin passing the word," Beta Dixon stated. "If other strangers are seen in town, we'll know about it immediately."

"Thank you, Beta Dixon," Jared replied respectfully. "I'll see you and the others shortly." He twisted his head a little so he could meet Carson's gaze and keep the phone in place. "Is the front door open, handsome?"

Carson nodded. "Unless this guy locked it," he added as he eased a hand towel underneath the injured man, pressing against the exit wound below his shoulder. "Want me to go check?"

"If you would."

Carson quickly pressed another towel beneath the man at his side, then placed another on top. After Jared said good-bye to Dixon, he rested his phone on the floor. Then he placed that hand on the stranger's side, pressing down on the wound.

Ignoring the groan that fell from the gunman's lips, Carson rose back to his feet. He bounded back upstairs and strode to the front of his house. Pausing in the front hall ten feet from the door, Carson saw the door was unlocked, just as he'd suspected.

He also noticed that the knob was turning.

Carson gritted his teeth as he sprinted from the hall. Skidding on bare feet, he nearly tumbled sideways as he rounded the table. He decided to go with it and rolled, allowing him to slide across the floor on the knees of his sweatpants.

Stopping at the corner of the table closest to the sliding

glass doors, Carson looked up . . . and spotted what he wanted. He grabbed the gun from the holster fastened under the bottom of the table. Jumping back to a crouch, he eased forward.

From Carson's vantage point in the dining room, he was just able to make out the edge of the front door. He eased the safety off his weapon as he watched the door ease slowly open. While he wasn't nearly as good a shot as his mate, he could generally hit was he was aiming at . . . especially at this distance.

Except, just then Carson noticed a red dot on the wall to the left of his head. Having lived with Jared and his obsession with guns for over a decade, he knew what that meant. Someone was trying to get a bead on him.

Good thing he gave himself away.

That meant whoever the shooter was either wasn't much of a shot, or he was inexperienced and overeager.

Either way, Carson capitalized on it.

Carson leaped forward. While he could possibly still be in the line of fire, he refused to be forced into a corner. As he heard the glass behind him shatter—*there goes the sliding glass door*—Carson spotted a man dressed in black streak through the slit of the open front door.

Son of a bitch!

Needing to warn Jared that hostiles were still in play—assuming the shattering glass hadn't done it—Carson shot wildly toward the front room.

Pop-pop-pop.

Then Carson hit the stairs, stumbling down the first few. He grabbed the railing with his free hand, stopping his wild momentum and wrenching his shoulder in the process. Hissing, he turned and slammed the door shut.

After slapping his palm onto a panel, which was disguised as every other piece of wood planking along that wall—locking the door—Carson turned to face his lover.

Jared crouched beside the downed gunman. The man's eyelids were slitted, and his features were pale. Sweat beaded his skin, but at least he was awake.

"Injun?"

Carson offered his mate a wry smile, then pinned a cold gaze on their injured guest. "You wanna tell me about your friends?"

The man's brows furrowed even as Jared growled and glared at the man. He began to reach down, probably to inflict pain, but the pounding on the door behind Carson made him pause. The man gasped upon hearing the noise, then glanced quickly between a clearly angry Jared and to Carson, who slowly descended the steps.

"I-I came alone," the guy practically wheezed. He coughed roughly as his gaze strayed to the door behind Carson. His voice remained raspy as he stated, "I don't know who those guys are."

"Son of a bitch," Carson grumbled as he rushed down the remaining stairs. "He's telling the truth."

Jared snarled, his hazel eyes dark with anger. "Damn." He pinned an angry glare on the door. "Guess that means torturing him for information is out."

"I have a name, Coleson," the guy grumped. "And we're sitting ducks at the bottom of the stairs."

Rolling his eyes, Jared strode across the large, rectangular room while saying, "I know." He stopped before an arrangement of bayonets and muskets that were hanging on the left side of the basement's wall. After twisting a bayonet in a clockwise movement to the right, Jared grabbed a musket hanging four feet to the left, then rotated it three-hundred-sixty degrees, causing the bayonet to pop back into place.

It also caused the third bookcase to the right to shift forward into the room and slide to the left. The entire right side wall was lined with bookcases full of reference books on a myriad of subjects. The secret room beyond was filled with Jared's more . . . questionable toys.

The room was also steel lined, damn near impregnable, and came with an escape tunnel.

While the people upstairs would be busy trying to break through the steel door at the top of the basement stairs, they could easily escape.

"If you don't mind carrying Kahlil, I'll get the bomb," Jared stated as he crossed to the table.

"Kahlil?" Carson watched Jared wave his hand at the downed and bleeding man. "You want to take him?"

Jared nodded as he began easing the bomb into a large, black duffel bag that had been resting on the floor under the workbench running the length of that wall. "Got a purpose for him. Yep."

Carson trusted his mate, so after bounding over the railing and landing lightly on the balls of his feet, he crouched beside the guy. "Shit," he grumbled, pausing.

"What?" Jared asked as he headed toward the door. "His leg isn't as bad as it looks, ya know." Pausing, he pointed toward Kahlil with his gun. "I actually only took out the outside flesh of his thigh right above his knee. Just looks bloody, and he'll have an impressive scar."

"Not that." Carson straightened and beckoned with his hand. "I need your phone."

Jared cocked his head, then immediately straightened. "Shit. Right." He shoved his gun into the shoulder holster he'd put on over his t-shirt. Carson knew his mate had those sorts of supplies stashed everywhere. "I'll call them. We need to move."

Carson nodded, accepting that. His mate's urging was intensified by the sound of someone attempting to blast through the door. The house trembled with the force of whatever the guys upstairs were doing.

Crouching again, Carson handed the first aid kit to Kahlil—just in case—then slid his arms under him.

"How do you expect to carry me?" Kahlil muttered.

His words were slurred, but Carson didn't hear much pain in them. Carson guessed Jared had given him pain meds from the kit while he'd been upstairs. From Kahlil's actions, Carson figured they were the pretty good ones that Lark had supplied them for emergencies.

"I'm stronger than I look," Carson stated, hoping to leave it at that.

Carson straightened, forcing Kahlil to curl against his chest. The man squeaked softly, then settled. After Carson had followed Jared into the back room, he stepped on a plate to the left of the doorway, causing the bookshelf to close behind him. He spotted his lover with his phone again pressed between his shoulder and ear. His mate was swiftly filling a couple more bags with everything from grenades to guns to rations.

Recognizing their pre-packed bug-out bag on the floor at Jared's feet, Carson knew they would have a couple of changes of clothes. It also explained where he'd gotten the clean t-shirt he currently wore. The bag over Jared's left shoulder and head contained an RPG—a rocket-propelled grenade launcher. Carson had never asked his mate how he'd acquired it.

Jared glanced over his shoulder at Carson, then winked as he stated into the phone, "Text me as soon as you've done a sweep. But make it quick. We don't have much time."

"Got it," Beta Dixon's voice came through the line.

Without another word to the beta, Jared straightened, allowing the phone to drop to the table. Then he slung a duffel over his right shoulder and picked up the duffel with his left. He walked over to one wall and grabbed a satellite phone off the shelf. After shoving it into his back pocket, Jared depressed a notch hidden at the base of a hanging diagram of a stealth jet.

The panel sank into the wall, revealing the escape tunnel.

"Shit. I shouldn't have been able to find you," Kahlil commented as they started down it.

"No, you shouldn't have," Jared replied. "You heard of a guy named Larson?"

Carson noticed the way Kahlil's brows furrowed. He appeared to be giving the question serious thought. Fighting back a smirk, Carson knew what his mate was doing.

What better way to question a suspect than when they were drugged and their defenses were compromised?

"Yeah," Kahlil replied slowly. "He's the guy who told Amelio Sanchez that a man matching the description of Coleson was hiding out in this area under the name of Jared." Snorting, he continued, "It's how I made the connection with the wire transfers on the Danner job."

"Larson," Carson snarled. "You were right."

Jared grunted. "I bet the girls' kidnapping was a ploy to draw me out of the mountains."

"What do you mean?" Carson asked.

Glancing over his shoulder, Jared explained, "It would be a lot easier to take me out in strange territory than on my own turf." He waved over his shoulder, indicating the house they were fleeing from.

Carson nodded, understanding.

It took them almost ten minutes to reach the end of the escape tunnel.

Jared placed all the bags he carried on the ground, then unholstered his weapon. Easing the concealed door open a crack, he peered out.

Carson wished he could be the one doing that, but he didn't trust Kahlil if he put him down not to go through their bags.

"Give me a minute," Jared whispered, then slipped out the door.

Rolling his eyes, Carson crept up to the door. He listened, but even with his shifter hearing, he wasn't able to make out anything except the natural night noises. After a moment, he heard the slightest rustle of fabric sliding along a leaf.

Carson tensed, but then relaxed again as the heady fragrance of his mate reached his nostrils.

"We're clear," Jared whispered.

Using his shoulder, Carson pushed the door open. He slipped out, then padded quietly to a nearby tree. Carefully, he eased Kahlil onto the ground.

Straightening, Carson peered down the hill. In the distance, he could just make out his home between the thick trees. The escape tunnel had brought them out about a mile away and up to a ridge, giving them the ability to survey the area.

Carson didn't see any movement below.

By the time Carson turned around, Jared had pulled out the RPG. He watched in surprise as his mate loaded it and hefted it onto his shoulder.

Jared offered Carson a pained smile. "Best cover your ears."

Lifting his hands on instinct, Carson watched in shock as Jared fired the weapon. He gasped as the grenade streaked through the air . . . straight at the home he'd shared with Jared for the last decade.

Within seconds, their sanctuary burst into flames.

CHAPTER SIX

Jared lowered the grenade launcher to the ground, suddenly too tired to hold it up. Casting a side-eyed glance Carson's way, he wrapped his arms around himself. He read the shock and disbelief in his wolf's eyes and prayed his man wasn't angry at his decision.

When Carson stepped close, Jared couldn't help but tense.

Carson sighed, then grabbed Jared and pulled him into a tight embrace. He dipped his head and nuzzled Jared's temple with his lips. When Carson rubbed one hand up and down Jared's spine and the other cradled his nape, he felt his tension begin to ease.

Sighing, Jared rested his cheek against Carson's chest.

For several long moments, they stood together like that, both watching their home burn.

"Are you angry?" Jared asked when he couldn't stand the silence any longer.

Carson scoffed softly. "No, my mate," he whispered before pressing a kiss to Jared's temple. "I do wish you'd have told me your plan, but I'm not upset."

Jared tipped his head up, and Carson met his gaze. His wolf's eyes were filled with concern, as well as a trace of sadness, but there was no anger there. Relief flooded him, removing the last hints of tightness in his shoulders.

Rubbing his hands over Carson's bare torso, Jared murmured, "Kiss me."

"Always and forever," Carson murmured, then lowered his head and did as Jared asked.

Carson rubbed his lips over Jared's, teasing and tasting. He kept the kiss light, a chaste reassuring meeting of lips. It felt as if Carson was making love to him with his mouth, and it sent a warm wash of tingles trickling through Jared's body.

After a few minutes of Carson sensually manipulating Jared's lips, he lifted his head. His wolf smiled down at him. "So? What's your next idea, my love?"

Jared's heart raced in his chest, and he sucked in a relieved breath. His heart swelled, and his body practically vibrated. He felt his dick twitch behind his fly, and he desperately wanted to feel his mate fill him.

Unfortunately, Jared was all too aware of the injured assassin propped up at the base of the tree ten feet away.

"Now, we use the bodies pulled from our burning home to stage our death." Jared tipped his chin in Kahlil's direction. "We ask Vince to change our friend's memory, and he gets the reward for taking me out." Seeing Carson's brows lift in obvious surprise, Jared continued, "Quick, clean, and gives us plenty of time to confirm the hits on my head are removed, my family is safe, and we can track down Castrose to find out if he accepted funds from one of the families Kahlil mentioned, or if there's a fourth player in this."

Carson nodded. "Sounds good." Then he peered back down the hill at the still-burning building. "What about the pack?"

Jared could guess at what Carson was asking. Sliding his hand up, he threaded his hands into his man's long, black hair. He tangled his fingers in the slick strands.

"They're still our pack. I've been in the area for ten years without aging," Jared pointed out. "How long has it been for you?"

Grunting, Carson narrowed his eyes. "Twenty-two. I see your point." Then he grinned. "Vacation?"

Laughing, Jared nodded. "Hell yeah. Once we get every-thing squared away, definitely a vacation."

Carson glanced Kahlil's way, and so did Jared. He spotted the glassy-eyed expression, and he knew the man was pretty out of it. Jared had purposefully given him a dose of shifter medicine so he wouldn't remember much and would be easy to question—half-dose, anyway. He didn't want the man's system compromised, after all.

After accepting one more kiss from Carson, Jared eased from his lover's arms. He pulled out the satellite phone and gave it to him. "If you don't mind giving Beta Dixon a call and asking him the ETA on when he should reach logging road B-seven, I'll ask Kahlil a few more question."

Carson took the phone as he nodded.

Jared crossed to where Kahlil was resting. His expression appeared serene, and he even smiled when Jared knelt before him. Yeah, he was pretty out of it.

"Tell me what you know about Scottson," Jared demand-ed, keeping his voice soothing. "Is he freelance? Or does he work for someone specific?"

Kahlil blinked at him. His words were slow to come and slightly slurred, but he answered. "Scottson works for the Mohamed family. Enforcer. Want you alive."

Jared could just bet why the rich family wanted him alive. Almost sixteen years before, he'd accepted a job to remove the head of the family's second son and extract his wife. Jar-ed had done it, removing the woman from an abusive, hell-hole of a life. Only he knew where he'd set her up.

Knowing she'd been pregnant at the time, Jared bet the family wanted the son she'd birthed.

Not in this lifetime.

"Well, it's a moot point now." Jared grinned widely. "Es-pecially since you killed me."

"Mmm-hmm . . ." Seeing Kahlil furrow his brows in con-fusion, he added, "You'll take my charred remains back to the Sanchez family and get your million dollars." Deciding to plant some further advice in the guy's drugged brain, Jared told him, "You don't make a very good assassin, Kahlil." The guy talked way too damn much. "Use the money to get out of the life and stick with computers."

"Had to pay for Mom's surgery," Kahlil mumbled.

Okay. That's interesting.

Jared made a mental note to keep track of Kahlil after he left — discreetly, of course.

"Did you get what you need from him?"

Tipping his head back, Jared peered up at Carson. "Yeah."

"Then do you still need the bomb?"

Jared smirked up at Carson. He could only imagine how uncomfortable it made his lover to be carrying around an explosive device. His wolf was a shifter, after all. He would prefer to use his teeth and claws as weapons . . . even if he did know how to use a firearm.

"Afraid so," Jared told him. "I still need to find Castrose to confirm what family he's working for."

Carson tipped his chin toward Kahlil. "He didn't recognize the name?"

Damn. Shoulda asked.

Jared focused on Kahlil and noticed his eyes were closed. He snapped his fingers. When that didn't get the man's attention, he reached out and checked his pulse. It was there but sluggish.

"We really need to get him to Lark," Jared mused. "While we've stopped the bleeding and I didn't hit him anywhere vital, he could probably use a blood transfusion." Peering up at Carson again, he asked, "How long until our ride comes?"

"If we start hiking now, we'll probably be there just as they arrive."

"Sounds great."

Jared had never had to run for his life before, even though

he'd always been prepared for it. Rising to his feet, he rested his hand on Carson's hip, rubbing his warm flesh with his thumb. "I'm sorry my past caught up like this, Injun."

Carson's thin lips curved into a wide smile, and his eyes gleamed with warmth as he met Jared's own. "My mate." He cradled Jared's cheek in one big palm and teased his thumb along the corner of Jared's mouth. "We knew there was a possibility of it happening. And now that it has, we will deal with it and move on. Done and done."

Before meeting Carson, Jared had never imagined that he could feel so much emotion for another person. This man, this wolf shifter, accepted him.

Jared swallowed as his throat began to clog and his eyes began to water. He blinked quickly as he swallowed twice. "I love you."

Carson's expression morphed into one of hunger, and his dark eyes smoldered. "Oh, my mate." He dipped his head until his lips were just a hairsbreadth from Jared's own before whispering, "And I love you, Jared. You are my everything."

Groaning, Jared surged up and captured Carson's lips. He slipped his tongue out and glided it across his lover's. Wrapping his arms around Carson, Jared gripped him tightly as he welcomed the ravishing his mate gave him.

Jared felt Carson's arms tighten around him, and he was pulled flush to his bigger lover. His senses sang, and he relished the heat of Carson's body seeping into his own. Jared groaned as his stomach clenched, his cock oozing behind the fly of his jeans.

Rocking his hips, Jared rutted against Carson's upper thigh. He noticed an answering hardness pushing into his lower belly. Then Carson must have spread his legs, for in the next instant, Jared felt his lover's erection grind against his own.

Moaning into Carson's mouth, Jared felt his balls tingle and roll, sending a delicious zing up his spine. Between the feel of his lover in his arms and the adrenaline from the fight and running, Jared knew he was primed. Even though he knew if he didn't stop now he would blow in his jeans, he couldn't seem to make himself stop.

"Damn, that's hot."

Carson snapped his head up, allowing Jared to suck in a much-needed lungful of air. Following his wolf's gaze, he spotted Kahlil still on the ground, but his eyes were open. He was cupping his crotch and massaging his clearly outlined erection.

Even the sight of the assassin who'd just tried to kill them getting off on them making out couldn't soften Jared. Hell, he couldn't even still his damn hips. With his mind clouded by lust, his one focus was getting off.

A growl escaped Carson. He didn't seem to have the same problem as Jared. His wolf lifted Jared into his arms and strode through the trees. On instinct, Jared wrapped his legs and arms around his mate.

"Get yourself off on your own," Carson grumbled as he cast a glance over his shoulder. "You got two minutes."

Jared peered back at Kahlil, who seemed to be taking Carson's words to heart. He already had his fly open and was fishing out a long, erect dick. While the meaty erection was a nice thickness, Jared didn't think it had anything on Carson's.

"Stop staring at Kahlil's cock, mate," Carson snapped.

Barking a laugh even as the view disappeared behind tree branches, Jared grinned at his lover. "You know you're the only one I want."

"Still don't need anyone else checking out your dick or mine, and looking at someone else's is damn different than porn."

Jared didn't understand how, but he didn't contradict Carson. His wolf's feral possessiveness gleamed from his dark eyes. Feeling his heart rate spike, he knew what was coming.

"There's lube in my hip pocket."

"Of course there is," Carson responded gruffly as he put him down. "Get it out, and then get your damn pants off."

Obeying quickly, Jared dug out the single-use packet of lube before shucking his boots and pants. Then he turned and bent, resting one hand on the tree. He held out the lube over his shoulder.

"Not like that," Carson countered even though he took the lube. Then he smacked Jared's ass, causing a wash of pleasant tingles to spark across his skin. "Turn around."

Doing as Carson bid, Jared turned. He rested his back against the trunk behind him. Gripping his dick with one hand, he cradled his balls with his other. He squeezed both, hard, doing his best to stem his need to come from the gorgeous sight before him.

Carson stood naked before him, the afternoon sun lighting up his bronze skin. He'd opened the lube packet and poured a good portion onto his prick. As Jared watched, he stroked his cock . . . up and down . . . up and down.

Spotting a bead of pre-cum gleaming at Carson's slit, Jared licked his lips.

A husky chuckle rumbled from Carson, causing Jared to snap his gaze back to his lover's face.

"Gods, I do love the way you look at me," Carson told him, a possessive grin curving his features. "And all mine."

Jared's breath hitched in his chest. His cock jerked in his hold. "Yours."

Carson growled low in his throat as he held out the open lube packet. "Hold this."

Somehow, Jared managed to release his balls and take the

packet.

As soon as his hands were free, Carson grabbed Jared's hips and lifted him off the ground. He kept Jared's back pressed against the tree, and Jared once again wrapped his legs around his lover's waist. Carson slid his left arm around Jared's hips, gripping his opposite cheek, then held out his right hand.

"Pour the rest of that onto my fingers, mate."

Anticipation thrumming through him, Jared was more than happy to comply. After squeezing as much fluid as he could onto Carson's fingers, he tossed the packet to the ground. Feeling his lover's fingers tease the wrinkled skin of his hole, Jared groaned roughly and grabbed at his wolf's arms for balance.

"Mine," Carson declared as he pushed in two fingers.

Jared moaned at the mild burn, which was quickly soothed by the warming lubricant.

"Yours," he repeated, rocking into Carson's stretching touch.

Carson didn't give him long to adjust. After only a few plunges of his fingers, he pulled them out.

Jared whined in dismay. His chute muscles spasmed, and he felt so damn empty.

"Please, Injun. Need you."

"Yeah you do," Carson agreed as he kissed the head of his dick to Jared's hole. "Just as I need you."

Holding Jared's gaze with his look of simmering lust, Carson thrust forward and sank deep into Jared's body.

"Yessss," Jared hissed, welcoming his lover. When Carson bottomed out, he paused, and Jared grinned at his man. "So perfect. Every fucking time."

CHAPTER SEVEN

Feeling the exquisite squeeze of Jared's chute muscles clamping onto his dick, Carson let out a long, low growl. His eyes narrowed, and he stared into his mate's eyes. The green dominated Jared's hazel eyes, betraying the lust his human felt just as sure as the tantalizing scent of his arousal did.

"All mine." Declaring that never grew old.

Jared grinned up at him. "And you're mine, Injun."

Carson grinned back. Hearing that never grew old, either.

With his erection buried within Jared's body, Carson's need to move became too much. He'd already been damn close to coming in his sweats like some untried cub. How his mate got to him each and every time still blew Carson's mind.

Easing his prick partway out, Carson groaned huskily. He immediately began pushing back in. Resting his forehead against Jared's, Carson began a slow thrust and retreat rhythm, sinking into his mate over and over.

"Oh, Jared," Carson muttered, the massage over the nerve endings on the sensitive skin of his erection causing his knees to grow weak. He locked his legs as he whined and picked up speed. "Need."

"Fuck me hard, my wolf," Jared encouraged. "I wanna feel you for days."

Carson chuckled roughly. "You'll feel me for days because I'm gonna fuck you several times this afternoon," he vowed. Then he sped up his strokes.

At the same time, Carson wrapped his hand around Jared's erection and began stroking in time with his ruts. He growled low in his throat as he felt his balls pull tight. Only his desire to have his lover come with him allowed him to stay his instinct to coat his mate's channel with his seed.

Jared's fingernails bit into the skin of Carson's arms, and he rocked his hips with each pass, meeting his every move. His human's open response sent Carson's senses soaring. Unable to resist, he sank his canines into Jared's flesh, his need to renew his bond, to assure his wolf that his mate was safe and with him, surging through him unchecked.

His mate's broken cry of bliss echoed amidst the trees.

Carson sucked on Jared's flesh as he sank his cock deep into the man. His prick pulsed as his balls unloaded. As he swallowed the nectar that was Jared's life-giving fluid, Carson poured his seed into his mate, soaking his channel and marking him inside and out.

"Injun," Jared mumbled into his ear. His hands loosened on his arms. "So damn good." Jared slid his palms up his arms to his chest, lightly scraping his nails across his flesh. Then he snickered. "Although, I bet by now we're going to be keeping Beta Dixon waiting."

Snorting, Carson eased his softened prick from Jared's channel even as he slid out his teeth. He lapped across his mate's flesh, sealing the wound, as he lowered him to the ground. Resting his hands on Jared's hips, Carson held him steady until he felt certain his lover had found his feet.

Lifting his head, Carson grinned at Jared. "Even if he's put out, it was worth it."

"Hell yeah, it was."

After pecking one last kiss to Jared's lips, Carson released him. He bent and grabbed his sweatpants, then pulled them on. Watching Jared slide his jeans up his legs, he brushed the bark from the back of his human's shirt.

"Are you okay?" Carson figured he'd been pushing his mate into the tree pretty hard. "Did I hurt you?"

Jared grinned broadly at him. "Only in the best damn way, Injun." Then he smacked Carson's ass and started back through the forest. "Come on. We got shit to do."

Carson followed his lover, unable to wipe his own smile off his face. Well, that was until Kahlil came into view. The man still rested against the tree, and he was once again unconscious. This time, however, his flaccid dick was in his hand, and the scent of spilled cum filled the air. A healthy spray of the white stuff was also spread before him.

Sighing, Carson shook his head.

Snorting, Jared commented, "At least he passed out from pleasure this time."

Unable to help himself, Carson barked a laugh. "I'll lift him, and you fix his pants."

"Oh, now I not only get to ogle another guy's dick, but I get to touch it, too?" Jared teased.

Carson growled. "Never mind. I'll do it."

Jared laughed and left him to it, heading back into the tunnel's exit.

Crouching next to Kahlil, Carson first checked his pulse. He found it. Next, he slid his left arm around the guy's torso, gripping the opposite side of his ribcage. Carson did his best to keep his hand well above where Jared had shot him near his left hip.

He eased the man forward and to the left, lying him flat on the ground.

While grabbing Kahlil's jeans with his right hand, Carson moved his left hand to the small of the man's back and lifted him just enough so he could slide them over the mounds of his ass. He got caught up for a second by forgetting about the man's underwear — shifters rarely bothered with that particular item of clothing. After he had everything back in place, Carson quickly zipped and buttoned his fly, then buckled his belt.

By the time Carson pivoted where he'd crouched, he saw that Jared had returned — once again carrying all the bags — and his lover was smirking at him.

Carson gave his man a mock scowl as he grumbled, "And I didn't have to touch his dick once."

Jared chuckled as he winked. "Let's get moving, Injun. Kahlil needs Lark's help, and I need to know what's going on with our place." Grimacing, Jared muttered, "And I need to know how our firefighters are doing controlling the blaze." He shook his head. "Glad it's still early spring. I'd hate to have started an uncontrolled burn."

Lifting Kahlil into his arms, Carson grunted. "Yeah, that would not be good, but our firefighters are good. Strong."

As they started through the woods, Jared glanced at Kahlil, then met Carson's gaze. "Is that because most of them are shifters?"

Carson chuckled softly. "Could be, but they are skilled. Well-trained."

"That they are."

After that, they fell silent as they hoofed it swiftly through the forest.

As Carson had guessed, it took them less than ten minutes to make it to the rendezvous point. As the trees parted and an old rutted logging road appeared, he spotted a flash of dark blue between the trees. A moment later, Carson realized it was a vehicle.

Carson saw Dixon leaning against the hood. His arms were crossed over his chest, and he was chewing on a toothpick. Dixon's focus was riveted at him even before they cleared the trees.

Once they were within thirty feet, Dixon pushed away from the vehicle. He pulled the toothpick from his mouth and used it to point at the man Carson carried. "That the guy who tried to kill ya?" he asked before sliding the toothpick into the front pocket of his flannel shirt.

"Yep," Jared immediately replied while pointing at the SUV. "This unlocked?"

"It is," Dixon replied as his gaze swept over them all. He openly sniffed the air before saying, "I would've asked what kept you, but I already know." Dixon turned away and headed toward the front seat. "Load up. I'll get you all to the alpha's place. The doc is waiting."

Jared opened the back door, then motioned for Carson to lay Kahlil on the bench seat. Then he rounded to the back and used his foot under the rear sensor to get the vehicle's back door to open. By the time Jared returned to the door, Carson had the front door open and motioned for his lover to climb in.

Shaking his head and waving his hand, Jared declined the offer. "Naw. You go ahead. I'm gonna climb in the back and make sure *Sleeping Beauty* doesn't cause problems." He grinned widely as he added, "And that he won't fall off the bench seat."

Carson snorted. Cupping Jared's nape, he pulled him forward. He pressed a hard kiss to his lips, then released his man, climbed into the front seat, and enclosed himself in the cab. While pulling on his seatbelt, Carson heard the door behind him close.

Dixon fired up the engine and started them moving.

"Did you blow up your house on purpose?" Dixon asked curiously, glancing from Carson, then to the rearview mirror at Jared. He returned his focus to the road while steering around a pothole. "Because of him?" Dixon jerked his chin toward the still-unconscious Kahlil.

"Not because of him," Jared claimed, leaning forward and resting his forearms on the back of the middle bench seat.

"We had Kahlil wrapped up when another group dropped in unannounced." He growled softly, showing a hint of his frustration. "As much as I would have loved to interrogate them, this seemed like the safer option for everyone attached to me." Meeting Carson's gaze, Jared added softly, "Besides, shifters have to remake their identity every few decades anyway, and this way, I can be sure not only my family is safe, but the pack is as well."

Dixon grunted. "Didn't think you had a noble bone in your body, Jared." He smirked as he glanced in the rearview mirror before returning his focus to the road. "Guess I was wrong."

"You're not wrong," Jared countered, his voice taking on an amused quality. "But you are family. That means I do whatever I can to keep you all safe."

Narrowing his eyes, Dixon scowled. "You know, you could have asked for help, Jared." He glanced Carson's way before adding, "We were already on our way. We could have helped take out the new arrivals."

Carson sighed even as he nodded. "Very true, but that would have potentially put the alpha-mate in danger."

Growling under his breath, Dixon nodded slowly. "Is that really the reason?"

"You wouldn't be spoiling for a fight, would you, Dixon?"

While Carson recognized Jared's teasing tone, Dixon obviously didn't. He growled low in his throat. Slowing the vehicle a smidge, he turned in his seat and glared at him.

"What the fuck is your problem?" Dixon demanded. "Ever since I joined the pack, you've been nothing but antagonistic to me. Don't think I don't know what you've really been thinking beneath your sickly sweet and pleasant facade."

Jared straightened in his seat. His eyebrows shot up, and

he flicked his gaze toward Carson. After Carson had offered the slightest of eyebrow lift, Jared returned his focus to Dixon.

Carson had known the altercation between Dixon and Jared would happen eventually. One wolf shifter would accept the leadership of another wolf simply because he was bigger, stronger, faster, and more aggressive. That was just the way of shifters.

Jared was human, however, and he didn't feel that way. His mate was just too self-assured and confident to roll over and accept another's authority without the man proving himself. Jared required evidence that Dixon was a suitable leader.

Since the pack was so large and Dixon was taking over his duties slowly—which gave him the time to learn about everyone in the pack and meet with them personally, with Alpha Declan by his side—Dixon hadn't yet gotten into a situation to prove himself.

"Okay, Dixon," Jared began, speaking slowly, obviously choosing his words carefully. "I'll be the first to admit that change is difficult for me." He flashed a smile Carson's way. "Hell, even with the mate-pull and a completed bond, it took me almost a month to move here to be with Carson."

Dixon's eyes widened, and he cast a shocked glance Carson's way. "A month?" he rumbled, his voice sounding pained. "What the fuck?"

Carson nodded as he shrugged. "The wait sucked, but it was worth it in the end."

"As far as what you thought was my sickly-sweet attitude," Jared continued, his smile holding more than a little bit of mischief. "That was me trying to be polite." He shrugged. "Obviously, I'm not very good at it."

Frowning, Carson shook his head. "You know how to be polite just fine," he countered, confusion filling him. He'd seen Jared polite on several occasions.

"Ah, but those were people I didn't give a shit about, and I had no plan to see them again." Jared heaved a sigh as he rested his forearms on the back of the middle seat once more. "Dixon, however. He's important to the pack, and I was trying to stay in line and put my best foot forward and not make waves."

Rubbing his palm over his face, Jared seemed to still be searching for the right thing to say—or maybe how to explain himself.

Carson wished he had chosen to sit back there. His desire to soothe and comfort his mate surged through him, hard to control. He wanted to hold Jared so damn bad.

"So, you're saying you were being extra nice and trying too hard, which made you come off as a self-righteous prick?"

Dixon's tone was dry, and his words were curt, and Carson just managed to bite back his growl.

"Exactly," Jared immediately replied. He grinned broadly. "And just so we're clear, I *am* an asshole to most people until they prove they deserve my respect." Then he shrugged. "Besides, I've always been a nerd at heart. Don't you know that nerds have no people skills? All mine were learned with the express purpose of manipulating people in my work as an assassin." Jared's cheeks actually took on a pinkish hue, betraying his discomfort even more than his slightly spicy scent. "With you and your situation, I had absolutely no idea how to act."

A slow smile curved Dixon's thick lips, and his blue eyes appeared to twinkle. "Now that we have that all cleared up, let's get you to the alpha's."

To Carson's surprise, that was all that was needed to clear the air between them.

CHAPTER EIGHT

For the next couple of days, Jared and Carson lay low. While Jared had had plenty of experience keeping out of sight and being reclusive when between jobs—back in the day—this was the first time he'd ever relied on others to help keep him safe. Tucked in Carson's arms, he slept at Alpha Declan's big lodge-style cabin.

One afternoon, Jared and Carson had been forced to hide deep in the woods for several hours. Evidently, due to the fact that Carson was in the employ of the human park ranger's department, one of the state's top officials had come out to review the report with Declan—who was Carson's direct superior.

From what Jared had heard, they'd spent time going over Carson and his partner's death. They'd also discussed the fact that the house appeared to have been blown up. Fortunately, that had been explained on a faulty valve on a propane storage tank that had been near the house.

The rest of the time Jared and Carson had managed to stay in the loop of what was going on.

As Jared had hoped, two corpses had been located in the remains. He had no idea who they were, but Lark had taken tissue and dental samples to attempt identification. There was a third man located fifty feet behind their home. He'd been knocked out of the tree he'd been hiding in by the blast—along with his sniper rifle—and had broken his neck on impact.

Jared had thought it a shame. He would have loved to

have had the chance to question him. Instead, Jared had to hope Kahlil's guess that those who'd infiltrated his home were led by Scottson and backed by Mohamed.

He supposed he would learn soon enough.

Speaking of Kahlil, Jared smiled as he greeted Frankie Drunger. The big wolf shifter entered Declan's home, a wide grin splitting his features. His vampire lover, Vince, was close behind and immediately wrapped his arm around Frankie's waist.

The pair hadn't been able to make it the previous day as Frankie had been working with his brother Reb at his tattoo parlor. After that, they'd been holding a birthday party for their son, Freddie. Jared and Carson would have normally gone to such an occasion, but recent events . . . well, that hadn't worked out for them.

"How was the birthday party?" Jared asked, smiling as he glanced between them. "Did Freddie enjoy the bouncy house?"

Since Jared and Carson had backed out at the last minute, Jared had ordered the delivery and assembly of not only a massive bouncy house but also a large inflatable slide.

Good thing Frankie and Vince had such a huge backyard.

Frankie's grin expanded even wider. His dark eyes lit up. He immediately began to nod.

"Freddie loved it! Thank you so much!" Then Frankie sobered. "I'm sorry about your house. We would have understood even without such a kind gift."

"It was my pleasure."

Jared had had to hack into a couple of databases, including his bank and the bouncy house company's bank. He'd managed it though. After that, all it had taken was a reminder phone call to the company, and they had scrambled to fulfill the order.

Frankie beamed, clearly having loved the gift for his

young son who'd just turned five.

After reaching out and slapping Frankie solicitously on the upper arm, Jared turned his attention to Vince. "I appreciate your willingness to come. I have a favor to ask."

Vince dipped his chin in a nod. "I'm always happy to help the pack."

Jared shook his head. "This isn't for the pack," he countered, needing to be blunt with the vampire. "This is for me."

Offering a negligent shrug as well as a mild smirk, Vince stated, "If it's for you and your safety, it's for your pack." Then his gaze drifted to Frankie and how he had begun regaling Carson with stories about how much Freddie had enjoyed the bouncy house and slide. The vampire's dark eyes held such warmth, that even when he returned his focus to Jared, it didn't all fade. "Besides, you brought my beloved and son hours of unexpected enjoyment. I'm happy to help if it's within my abilities."

Dipping his head in a nod, Jared accepted that at face value.

"I need you to look at a human male and tell me if you can alter his memories. I need the changes to be fairly specific." Upon seeing Vince lift a brow, betraying his interest, Jared shrugged. "I need him to report my death to his superiors. There has to be details, or he won't be believed."

Vince nodded. "Okay. Take me to him, and I'll see if I can put him in a trance."

"Thank you."

Ever-so-slowly, Vince's lips curved into a wide grin until his fangs peeked between them. "Did you just say thank you?"

Jared narrowed his eyes.

Laughing softly, Vince murmured, "Hearing that was worth anything." When Jared rolled his eyes, Vince nudged his elbow into his arm, gaining his attention. "I'm just giving you shit, my friend. Let's go."

Nodding, Jared returned his attention to Carson. He touched his mate's shoulder, drawing his focus. Jared didn't even have to ask. All he had to do was meet his wolf's eyes.

Carson dipped his head and pecked his lips to Jared's. "Holler if you need anything."

Jared nodded. "I will."

Then Jared led the way out of the front room and toward the back. He nodded at Sara, who was in the kitchen preparing dinner. Jared figured she cooked because she needed something to focus on other than Ricky.

As far as Jared could tell, Ricky still remained distant, but at least he talked to her when they were in the same room. Jared had even seen them chatting for a few minutes on the back deck the evening before. He knew Kontra's gang was supposed to get in that afternoon, so he hoped Draven would have some tips to help move the pair forward even further . . . or faster.

Whatever.

Jared just hated seeing Sara hurting.

Too bad I can't knock the man upside the head. That'll just piss off the girl.

Dismissing the idea, Jared led the way up the stairs and down the hall. He paused at the second to last door on the left and knocked lightly. When he didn't get a response, he knocked a second time.

Jared grumbled under his breath, then gripped the knob and entered. Sweeping his gaze over Kahlil's still form, he saw his eyes were closed and sweat beaded on his aristocratic brows. The dark-haired man's features remained at ease, however, indicating that he slept.

At least he wasn't ignoring my knock.

Easing to the left of the doorway, Jared crossed his arms over his chest. "This is Kahlil Almasi. He tried to assassinate me, but it didn't work out so well for him." He scoffed softly as he eyed the injured man.

"So what? You want him to forget he found you? Forget you exist?" Vince closed the door behind them, then leaned against it while shoving his hands into his pockets. "Won't that just mean another will come after you? Or am I supposed to delve into his mind and find out who has a hit out on you?"

Jared shook his head. "None of the above."

Before Vince could question him, Jared quickly explained what he wanted. He also told how Lark had put an extremely discreet tracking chip in the back of Kahlil's shoulder. That way they would know when the man returned *Jared's* burnt body to the Sanchez organization. Lark was even forging paperwork, complete with tissue samples, so there would be no question of Jared's death.

Then Jared intended to track the filtering of the information so he could verify that all the other organizations' hits were removed from his various aliases.

"So, you don't have a problem with him earning a million dollars from your head?"

Jared shrugged as he focused on the fairly handsome man lying in the bed. "He was doing a job. Even though he botched it up, he gave me information." Peering at Vince, he narrowed his eyes. "Invaluable information. Not only can I reward him for his sacrifice, but I can benefit from it, too."

Grimacing, Jared muttered, "And my family will be safe as will my pack."

Vince nodded slowly as he crossed to the foot of the bed. "Do you plan to go to your funeral?"

Shock flooded Jared, and he cocked his head as he scowled at Vince. "No. Why would I do that?"

Turning to face him, Vince shrugged one shoulder. "I went once." The corner of his lips curved into a wry smile. "I *am* almost two hundred years old. I was curious." Narrowing his eyes, he tipped his head up and stared at the ceiling. "While I didn't have too many human friends, it was still an interesting experience." Vince blinked once, twice, then turned his head and focused on Jared. "I know you're damn good at disguises, so you might consider going." His smile turned sad. "If for no other reason than getting to see your family one last time before exile forces you to stay away from them for over a decade."

Jared gaped. He hadn't really thought of it like that. His decision to take out his house had been rash . . . even if Carson was close to needing to rebuild his identity. Jared had only thought of his family's safety. Nothing else had been a consideration and certainly not how losing him so abruptly would affect them.

Damn.

Just as fast as Jared began to second guess himself, his tension settled. Even now, he knew he wouldn't change his choices. Just as surely as he knew his past would someday catch up with him, Jared knew his death to the world was inevitable.

"I'll consider that," Jared murmured, nodding in thanks. Leaning against the wall, he pointed a finger at Kahlil. "And this one?"

Vince twined his fingers, then cracked his knuckles. "Let's take a look."

As Jared watched Vince round the bed, he saw the vampire's irises bleed to a blood-red color. Vince leaned over the bed and touched the guy's temple. Kahlil's eyes opened as he gasped, and just that fast, he stilled as he stared transfixed into Vince's eyes.

Jared hadn't ever had a chance to watch a vampire work, and he found it fascinating. As he watched, both men's pupils retracted to tiny points, causing their irises to dominate their eyes. Kahlil's face blanked as his lips grew slack.

Vince's eyes narrowed just a smidge.

Then Vince's low voice filled the room. With clear, concise sentences, he gave Kahlil his new memories. Vince even went so far as to explain away all the man's bullet wounds, describing one hell of a fight between them, which ended in a gas explosion that Kahlil barely managed to get clear of.

That, at least, would explain why it took a bit of time for Kahlil to recover and return to the Sanchez's with Jared's body.

Jared appreciated the vampire's ingenuity.

Finally, Vince murmured, "You will sleep for three days, then wake in a private clinic under an assumed identity. You will sneak out and finish your mission." Vince grinned as he added, "You will care for your family . . . unless they're abusive or bigoted."

Slapping a hand over his mouth, Jared tried not to snort with laughter at that last bit. He bit his tongue in order to do it. Swallowing hard, he felt relief that he hadn't drawn blood.

That would just send Carson into a frazzle.

Vince finally blinked once, twice, then glanced Jared's way. With his eyes still blood red, the vampire smirked at him. "Did I miss anything? Anything you want to add?"

Jared shook his head. "No. Wow." He snorted. "Damn, buddy. You're good."

As Vince waggled his brows and grinned broadly, showing off his fangs, his eyes slowly returned to their normal blue color. "Yes, I am, but that's not what I asked."

Scoffing, Jared shook his head. "Okay, big head. Let's go."

Turning, Jared opened the door and slipped out of the room. "I need to go tell Lark that Kahlil will be sleeping for the next three days so he doesn't get worried." Noticing that Vince followed, closing the door behind him, Jared added, "And thank you. I do appreciate it. I don't want anything to lead back to the possibility of me still being alive."

"Then you need to take out Larson."

Jared paused and cocked his head, narrowing his eyes at the vampire, wondering if he knew something.

Vince rolled his eyes as he crossed his arms over his chest. "Larson knows you're mated with a shifter, Jared," he pointed out, his expression growing serious.

Nodding slowly, Jared mused, "Then we need to make certain Carson's death is just as iron-clad as my own."

Dipping his head in a single deep nod, Vince silently agreed.

Before Jared could come up with anything else to say, he saw Ricky arrive at the top of the stairs at the end of the hall. The human paused, and his eyes narrowed a little. He nibbled his bottom lip for just a second, almost as if he were contemplating something. Then he started forward, crossing to the first door on the left.

After another glance in their direction, Ricky disappeared into his room.

Vince shoved his hands into his pockets as he let out a soft sigh. "Is Ricky still being an ass?" the vampire all but whispered.

Jared lifted his hand, palm down, and waved it in a *so so* motion. "They've started exchanging pleasantries," he replied softly, concern for Sara still riding him hard. "Slow but steady."

"I wonder if I could trance him to make him accept—"

Snorting, Jared lifted a hand as he shook his head. "Probably not the best idea." When he spotted the questioning look on Vince's face, he shrugged. "I already offered to tie Ricky to Sara's bed until he agreed to talk with her, but she kyboshed that idea." Smirking upon seeing Vince's parted lips and sagging jaw, Jared added, "I kinda think she wouldn't take too kindly to you messing with her mate's mind if something as simple as her mate tied to her bed caused her such . . ."

"Alarm?" Vince guessed when Jared didn't finish his thought.

Jared shook his head. "Alarm is definitely not the word I would use."

Vince scowled. "Then what?"

Mirth filling him, Jared grinned widely. "Possessiveness."

The vampire laughed. "The guy doesn't have a chance."

Jared chortled softly as he nodded. "I agree."

CHAPTER NINE

Just when Carson noticed Jared striding down the stairs from where he sat in the dining room chatting with Frankie, he heard the unmistakable sound of at least a half dozen motorcycles. He swiftly rose to his feet and rounded the table, grabbing his lover's hand. With a gentle tug, Carson tucked his mate against his side.

"Looks like the gang is here," Carson murmured.

Jared grinned cheekily, waggling his brows. "It's about damn time."

Carson laughed even as he nodded.

As they made their way to the front of the house, Carson spotted Alpha Declan, Beta Dixon, and Lark exiting the alpha's large office in the downstairs wing. He dipped his head in a nod of deference, and his wolf relaxed when his alpha offered a small smile and nod in return. Even Frankie, Vince, and Sara joined them as they all headed out onto the front porch.

Just as Carson had suspected, no less than ten motorcycles rolled into the huge front yard. As their drivers parked their bikes, he leaned against the railing while tucking Jared against his side. Carson recognized nearly all of the riders.

Most notable was the gang's alpha, a grizzly bear shifter named Kontra Belikov. He sported a massive six-foot-five frame with silver flecks through his dark-brown hair and goatee. The man had a network of connections all over the country, since the shifters in his motorcycle gang had found their partners all over the country.

Kontra's shifters were made up of a variety of shifters. There was the short, twink-like penguin shifter named Yuma all the way up to the thick and scarred beta of the gang, a Texas longhorn bull shifter named Sam. They even had a doctor python, an enforcer warthog, and so many more in between.

The man that they really needed help from, however, he was a fair-haired, slender vampire hybrid. While Draven needed blood to survive—his wolf shifter mate's blood—he also had the ability to cast spells. The man was considered a warlock, and unlike a circle of witches, warlocks didn't normally band together. Instead, they had mentor-student relationships, allowing them to teach their skills to another.

Draven had joined up with the gang when he'd led them to San Francisco so he could train Kontra's mate, Tim. They'd been together for a few years, so Carson guessed the man was learning the tricks of the trade.

For a few minutes, everyone traded greetings and platitudes, including Alpha Declan welcoming Alpha Kontra into his territory for as long as he wished. Sara put her fingers to her lips and let out a shrill whistle, catching everyone's attention. Grinning broadly—although to Carson it appeared a bit forced—she announced the noon-day meal, and everyone trooped inside.

The food was fantastic.

Carson always loved a good cheesy hash brown casserole. Plus, bacon and eggs never got old. Adding mushrooms, peppers, black olives, and a little cheese to the scrambled eggs just made them epic.

On top of that, there were biscuits with sausage gravy. Sara had also made banana pancakes, sausage links, and heavily buttered toast. A plentiful supply of thick maple syrup, peanut butter, honey, butter, and a variety of jams had already been laid out on the table.

Since there were too many people to all eat at the table, Alpha Declan opened the back door. The group trooped through the kitchen and dining room, filled their plates, then filed outside. The sun on Carson's face felt fantastic as he took a seat next to Jared and chowed down on the delicious food.

"Well, dang! It smells amazing around here," a melodious tenor called.

Carson lifted his focus from his plate and spotted Raul standing in the open doorway leading to the dining room. Behind him stood his wolf shifter mate, Sean, who held the hand of Lily, his six-year-old niece. They were raising the girl as their daughter, since her mother had died in childbirth.

"There's plenty if you want some," Alpha Declan called, waving his fork toward the interior of the home. "Grab a plate and come join us. Brahms should be here soon, too. He called earlier to tell me he received the fire inspection report from Inspector Usher."

Upon hearing that, Carson called, "Is Boyd Usher coming, too?"

If the man was, Carson knew he and Jared would have to make themselves scarce. While Brahms, the fire chief, was a wolf shifter in the pack, Boyd was not. He was a human who lived in Stone Ridge with his wife and four kids.

Since Carson and Jared were supposed to have died in the fire, if the Fire Inspector learned that they were still alive and well, the situation could get awkward fast.

Alpha Declan tipped his head, then winced and admitted, "He didn't say, but better safe than sorry."

Sean, Lily, and Raul joined them on the deck, crossing to where Carson and Jared sat. "We already ate, Alpha," Sean told him respectfully. "But thank you for the offer."

The blond wolf shifter had relocated to the pack when

Lily was an infant, joining them so he could claim his mate, Raul. Although Raul was human, since he'd moved there years before when Jared did and knew about shifters, he was an honorary member of the pack. Sean's old alpha had been very heavy-handed and controlling, and Sean always showed deep deference to those in the inner circle.

"We'll head into the woods then," Carson stated as he speared his last bite of sausage link.

"Could we borrow you, Draven?" Jared called to the vampire who was sitting on a bench seat beside Ricky.

The pair had been talking in low tones, but upon hearing his name, Draven turned and focused on Jared. "Borrow me?"

Jared nodded. "We could set up whatever you need out in the forest. I still need that human's location."

"There's no guarantee of success, but I'm happy to try," Draven told him.

"What are you doing?" Tim piped up, glancing between them. The man was Kontra's mate and also a powerful warlock.

Carson knew Jared hadn't asked the man for help out of respect for his position.

Draven didn't seem to have that compulsion. "I'm going to take an item that belonged to a human and attempt to use it to locate him." The vampire waggled his pale-blond brows. "Would you like to join me?"

"Hell yeah." Tim turned to look at the huge male sitting next to him, whose arm happened to be wrapped around his waist in a possessive hold. "I can go do that while you talk alpha shop with Alpha Declan. You don't mind, do you, Kontra?"

"Not at all, love," Alpha Kontra answered. "Go have fun." He dipped his head and pressed his goateed lips to Tim's, kissing him deeply before straightening and moving his arm. Then Kontra turned his attention to Declan. "Do you mind if my people head into your woods? We've been on the road a while, and it'd be good to stretch our legs."

Alpha Declan swept his dark-skinned hand in a grand gesture toward the pines abutting his backyard. "Not at all. Enjoy yourselves." He hesitated a second, then added, "Stay away from the North Pine Trail. I hear the youth pastor of a church located in Colin City brought a group of teenagers out for an overnight adventure."

Kontra nodded. "Got it. I'll *Google* it."

"You don't have to," Alpha Declan countered.

Even as Declan spoke, Lark bounced from his seat. "I'll get the local map. It's so much easier to understand than scrolling around a tiny screen." Then the doctor hurried into the house.

After that, the group seemed to scatter.

Carson returned to the bedroom to grab the duffel bag with the bomb in it. When he returned to the deck, Jared, Raul, Draven, and Tim were all waiting at the edge of the backyard. While he lifted a brow upon seeing Raul, he didn't question it since Jared was in the middle of telling his friend everything that had happened.

Raul's freckled face sported a dark flush, and his green eyes sparked with aggression. "Do you think they're going to connect me to you?" he asked as they hiked, worry filling his tone.

Understanding flooded Carson. Raul had worked with Jared for years, occasionally acting as his spotter or gathering intelligence for him. If someone had discovered who Jared was, Raul's life and that of his family could also be in danger.

"Kahlil never mentioned you, but we should definitely remember to ask Vince," Jared told him. "He was in the man's brain altering his memories. I bet he would have noticed if your name was attached to me in Kahlil's mind."

Raul nodded, his brows furrowing in agitation. "Thanks, man," he stated, lifting his arm with his fingers in a fist.

Jared did the same, and they bumped forearms. Then Raul turned and began jogging back the way they'd come.

"God, I feel bad for possibly bringing trouble Lily's way," Jared muttered, scratching his fingers over his scalp.

"Not Sean's way?" Tim asked curiously, lifting a brow.

Shrugging, Jared replied, "Sean's a wolf shifter with a slightly heightened sense of wariness from growing up in his home pack in Idaho." His lips twisted as he obviously thought about the group still up there. "Even being here for six years hasn't caused it to completely dissipate. Once Raul warns him, Sean will be on his toes."

As Tim nodded, his brows furrowing in thought, Draven asked, "What happened to that pack in Idaho? Didn't their alpha get removed?"

Carson nodded. "He did. So did the entire inner circle. When a new alpha and beta took over the pack, some pair from back East, we kept an eye on them for a while." Meeting Draven's gaze, he added, "Kyle still has to drive close to that area for his truck runs. They never appeared to care, so we stopped two years ago. There seemed to be no point in wasting the man-power."

"Will this clearing work?" Jared asked, turning and walking backward across the ten-by-fifteen oval space. He threw his arms wide in indication.

Draven nodded as he walked around the space. "This will work just fine." He pointed at a spot on the ground closer to the right side of the oval clearing. "Place the device there, then you all should stay well over to the other side."

Carson did as he'd been told and placed the duffel on the ground. "Do you need it removed?"

"Yes. Otherwise, the spell could get confused by the bag's

owner."

With careful precision, Carson removed the bomb from the bag, then took the duffel and crossed to the other side of the clearing where Jared sat with his back against a tree. He placed the bag on the ground, then sat beside his mate. Reaching out, he threaded their fingers together before bringing Jared's hand to his lips to give it a kiss.

Jared flashed him a smile, then returned his focus to the warlocks. Carson did the same.

Having only seen magick in action a couple of times, Carson found the process fascinating. The warlocks used dried herbs to manipulate . . . whatever it was that they did. Did they call it the ether? Carson realized he might have to ask.

Draven sat cross-legged on the ground, and Tim mirrored him. The device rested between them. After pouring several piles of dried herbs — one at each corner of the bomb — the pair of warlocks lifted their hands with their palms out and toward the disarmed explosive. The men shared a glance, then they both started speaking — chanting, really — so softly that even with his shifter hearing Carson couldn't make out the words — or maybe he just didn't understand them.

As Carson watched, both men's eyes lost focus. For quite a while, other than the flicking of their glazed-eyed gazes going this way and that, neither man moved. Carson didn't know how long it took, but it was long enough that he had to shift his weight because his butt was going to sleep. Finally, just as abruptly as they'd started chanting, they stopped.

Both men blinked once, twice, and the glazed expressions cleared. Tim grimaced as he lowered his arms. He stared at the bomb distastefully while rubbing his upper arms as if trying to warm himself.

Draven shook his head as he peered toward Carson and Jared. "That man has way too much time on his hands. The sheer size of his workshop. Just damn!" Heaving a sigh,

Draven flopped onto his back and stretched out his arms and legs. "You'd be jealous, Jared. Especially since all your shit just went boom."

"Maybe I'll take some of his stuff as my own," Jared replied dryly. "So you were able to locate him?"

Turning his head on the grass to glance between them, Draven nodded. "Yes, but it'll take some doing to get there. The man's a recluse."

"And Castrose has a huge network of traps and alarms," Tim chimed in, wincing. "It won't be easy to get through them, and if we hit anything, he'll have plenty of time to make his escape."

"Okay. So where is he?" Jared demanded.

Carson heard the impatience creeping into his mate's tone, so he added, "Please, guys. Give it to us straight. Where is Castrose Zukan holed up?"

Lifting up on his elbows, Draven told them, "The forest of Romania."

"Shit," Jared grumbled, drawing out the word while rubbing at his temple. He grinned suddenly as he turned to meet Carson's gaze. "Hey, that's actually somewhere I've never been." He bumped his shoulder into Carson's. "Vacation, Injun."

Carson chuckled as he grinned in response. "Sure, babe. Vacation." He turned his attention to the warlocks. "Any way I can talk you two into coming? We could use the help."

"We'll have to talk to Kontra and Vail," Tim began slowly, glancing Draven's way as if for reassurance. After Draven nodded, Tim smiled widely. "But, hell. I've never been there either. When did you want to leave?"

To Carson's surprise, Jared stated, "Not until after the funeral."

"Really?" Carson murmured, dipping his head close to his mate. "You want to go to your own funeral?"

Jared's eyes held a wealth of sadness as he explained, "Vince pointed out that it could be the last time I see my family in over a decade or even more." He sighed. "I know I won't be able to talk to them or anything, but it would be nice to at least have that much."

Carson couldn't imagine how Jared was feeling on the matter. While the man had lived away from his family when he was in his twenties and some of his thirties, Jared had done it on purpose. That had been to keep his family safe from his work, too.

Just like now.

As Carson nodded, he absently wondered if there was a way to allow Jared's family to know the truth. Except, would that make things worse? After all, Jared would outlive his family by centuries.

Perhaps this is for the best. After all, he still has his pack family.

CHAPTER TEN

R icky heard the voices before he spotted them. Using the masculine murmurs as a guide, he finally found the clearing where Draven was sitting with a few others. He had been told that Draven and Tim were performing a spell, but he was glad he'd missed that.

Not sure I'm ready to see magick again, yet.

Having seen a witch battle Draven, Tim, and their shifter buddies once, Ricky felt that was enough.

"Hey, Draven," Ricky called, waving a hand in greeting. "You got a few?"

"Sure, man," Draven responded, then waved at the grass near him. "Cop a squat."

Ricky snorted as he began crossing the distance between them. He nodded a greeting to the other men as he did so. When he reached Draven, he settled on his ass in the grass with one leg folded partly under him and the other knee cocked up for him to lean his forearms on.

Ricky opened his mouth, intending to ask for the reason he'd come to find him, but then his focus fell on the device sitting between Draven and Tim. "Holy fuck!" he cried, straightening. "Is that a bomb?"

Draven chuckled as he nodded. "Yeah."

"What the hell are you all doing with it?" Ricky hadn't meant for his tone to sound accusatory, and he winced when he realized it had. When he heard Jared's snort, he lifted a hand in placation as he quickly added, "Your house just blew up, so it's just a shock. Sorry, man."

Jared just offered a predatory smile in return.

Ricky wasn't offended. He knew the man had a reputation for being kind of an asshole. Plus, since Ricky had been giving Sara such a hard time about the whole mate thing, he knew he wasn't on Jared's *to be nice to* list.

After all, Sara considered Jared an honorary uncle . . . or so he'd heard.

Right. Sara.

Once again, Ricky opened his mouth, intending to ask for help, but Draven beat him to speaking.

"It's been disarmed, Ricky." Draven reached over and patted his knee reassuringly. "I used it to track down the location of the maker."

"Damn! You can do that?" Ricky couldn't hide his surprise.

"If I have a name and something of the person's that's important enough to them, yes," Draven claimed. His hand swept toward the device. "In this case, Castrose Zukan considers all his bombs a little like his children. He's proud of them, spends plenty of time on each, and when they go boom, he feels pride at that, too."

"That is . . . wow," Ricky muttered. "The help that could be on the force." He scowled at him. "Hey. How come you never did that with any of our bomb cases?"

Draven smirked. "How do you know I didn't?"

Ricky gaped, realizing that their high success rate could have easily been attributed to Draven's abilities. He knew he'd been given a bit of flack over the years after the man had left. His rate of case closure, as well as the speed of closure, had definitely dropped.

Ruffling his dark hair, Ricky tried not to think about how Draven had probably been carrying his ass. It wasn't a nice thought. Instead, he once again focused on his reason for hiking out there.

"Okay. Well, thank you," Ricky began, trying to be diplomatic. "But, uh, I actually came out because I was wondering if you could help me find Sara."

"Find Sara?" Draven repeated, his confusion evident. He waved toward the device. "You mean like I just did with the bomb?"

"Is Sara missing?" Carson asked, sitting forward as he scowled at Ricky.

Ricky quickly shook his head. "Oh, no. At least, I don't think so. She's out running." He waved his hand vaguely at the forest. "Somewhere." Focusing on Draven, Ricky cleared his throat. "I was told that since you're a vampire, you can speak telepathically with Vail. He's out there running, too. I thought he might know where and could direct me." He pointed at the satchel he'd set down beside him. "I thought a picnic with my mate would give us time for us to, uh, get to know each other." Ricky felt his face heat just saying that.

"First time admitting Sara is your mate out loud?" Jared asked, proving he was way too insightful.

After clearing his throat, Ricky nodded. "Yeah."

Jared's smile actually turned understanding . . . and maybe even a little sympathetic. "I had the same reaction when I pulled my head out of my ass." He reached over and threaded his fingers through Carson's hair, then used the hold to get his man to lean over.

Their kiss wasn't chaste, and Ricky felt his cheeks flush for a whole different reason. He turned away as he rubbed the back of his neck. While Ricky was better at accepting displays of affection between men, it still made him uncomfortable.

"Yes, that is true," Draven stated, drawing Ricky's attention. "I can indeed speak telepathically to Vail. Let me see where he is."

Ricky appreciated the distraction, because out of the corner of his eye, he could see that Jared had shoved Carson back on the grass and was now half-sprawled over him. Jared had his hand under Carson's t-shirt and was openly feeling him up. The soft grunts as they ate at each other's faces were really . . . distracting.

He didn't understand why neither Tim nor Draven said anything to the men.

Is this behavior normal?

"Hmm . . . Vail says a number of shifters are playing in a waterfall near an abandoned logging camp." Draven smiled at Ricky. "Sara is amongst them."

"I know where that is." Carson's deep voice announced that they'd come up for air. "I can take you."

Ricky turned his attention to Carson and opened his mouth, intending to thank the man. Except, right then, the wolf shifter reached down and adjusted his blatant erection. Feeling his cheeks heat once more, Ricky stared at the ground.

After swallowing hard, Ricky managed to mutter, "Thank you."

Draven's hand appeared in his line of sight, and Ricky looked up in surprise. All the other men were already standing. He took his friend's hand and allowed the vampire to pull him to his feet.

Clapping him on his back, then using the hold to start Ricky walking in the direction Carson and Jared were moving, Draven told him, "You will have to get used to public displays, my friend." His voice was low as he continued, "Shifters are very tactile, and once you complete your bond with Sara, you'll come to understand why all the couples are always touching each other in some way or another."

Ricky glanced Draven's way, grimacing when he saw the amused gleam in his friend's blue eyes. "It's been hard enough to keep my hands to myself now," he muttered out of the side of his mouth. He didn't want everyone to hear. "You sayin' it's gonna get worse?"

Draven laughed as he nodded. "Probably. For a while anyway." Then he pointed at the pair they were following. "And you'll have to get used to them, too. They're part of Sara's family. The whole pack is, and there are a lot of homosexual couples around here."

Ricky nodded absently, allowing his thoughts to consume him for a few minutes. After Tim split off, waving goodbye, and headed back toward the lodge and most likely Kontra, something else that had been bothering him floated through his mind. He grimaced, struggling with how to voice it.

"Just spit it out, Ricky," Draven encouraged.

Sighing, Ricky pointed at Carson and Jared. "They just faked their deaths, right?"

Draven nodded.

"And I figure since I'll be living so long, I'll have to do the same at some point."

Again, Draven nodded.

"You all didn't do it for me already, right?" Ricky blurted out, rubbing the back of his neck. "I've heard it's been done to others."

"You didn't ask them?" Draven's brows shot up, and his eyes widened, displaying his surprise.

Ricky cleared his throat before admitting, "I was kinda afraid to ask."

Draven barked a laugh, then called up to Jared and Carson, relaying the question.

Carson slowed his steps as he peered over his shoulder at him. He shook his head. "No, we didn't do that. You're on leave for a family emergency though." The man's even white teeth flashed as he grinned at him. "Your sister broke her leg."

"I don't have a sister," Ricky immediately replied. His only family was Rueben, who he'd seen earlier for the first time in years. They'd grown closer in the time that his brother had bonded with his shifter lover, Lamar, but he still felt more comfortable sharing his problems with Draven.

"We know." Jared waggled his brows as he told him, "You're half-siblings, and you were estranged, and now you're mending your relationship while helping your sister get back on her feet. It would make for a perfect excuse to quit your job and move here after you bond with Sara."

Ricky froze mid-step, nearly landing on his face.

Draven grabbed his upper arm, stabilizing him. "You really should have already thought about that," Draven whispered into his ear.

As Ricky started moving again, he nodded.

Yeah. I really should have. Now what?

Sara pranced amidst the shallows of the river. Her cloven hooves sank into the mud under the several inches of water, and with each step, when she pulled them back up, she made certain to splash the others in the water. The massive Bengal tiger—Detective Grady Stryker in animal form—used his paw to swipe her right back.

A blast of water suddenly doused them both, and Sara froze in shock. Turning her horned head, she spotted Grady's partner, Doctor Gordon Digby, lumbering toward them. His animal form easily parted the water as he dipped his trunk into the water once more.

In response to Gordon's attack, Grady roared and launched toward his lover. He twisted his large feline body so he landed broadside in the water. The resulting wave nearly crested over Gordon's head.

Gordon lifted his trunk and blasted him again.

Instead of retaliating against Gordon, Grady offered a chuffing rumble and paddled close enough toward shore to stand. Then he used a paw to splash a wave toward a log half suspended over the water. The water cascaded over the huge monitor lizard sunning himself there.

Detective Lyle Sullivan in animal form lifted his head and let out a long hiss, showing off row upon row of wickedly sharp teeth.

The tiger just chuffed again and lifted his paw once more.

"You know, if I didn't know about shifters, this would seem really strange to me."

Sara whipped her head around and peered at the man standing on the shore. Upon seeing Ricky there, she practically vibrated as need surged through her. Even in animal form, her blood heated and her breathing quickened.

"Hi, Sara," Ricky greeted, his lips curving in an uncertain smile. "Hope you don't mind. Carson brought me over." He used a thumb to point over his shoulder, indicating the trio of men—Carson being one of them. "I brought a few things." Ricky hefted the bag he carried. "Can I talk to you?" His gaze drifted to the other animals before returning to her. "Alone, maybe?"

Lyle immediately turned and slunk into the trees. Gordon and Grady began moving toward shore. Grady paused near Ricky long enough to bare his canines.

Even though Sara knew Grady wouldn't hurt Ricky, and she knew the big cat shifter was only warning him to behave or be nice or something similar, seeing Ricky stepping back in alarm raised Sara's own shifter instincts. She bounded out of the water and skidded to a stop between the two. Grady chuffed softly, and when Gordon popped him on the flank with his trunk, he began moving again.

"Here." Carson left a cell phone on a tree stump. "Call if you need anything."

Sara bobbed her head. Within the next moment, everyone else had slipped into the trees. The feel of Ricky's hand on her shoulder nearly caused her to start in surprise.

"You know, I've never seen a gazelle before," Ricky

murmured, rubbing his hand over her damp fur. "You really are absolutely stunning."

After just a second of hesitation, Sara reached out with her neck and nuzzled her head gently against Ricky's upper arm. She wasn't certain why he was actually out there, but his touch felt too good to resist. When Ricky slid his hands to either side of her furred cheeks, cradling her head and rubbing with his fingertips, Sara wanted to purr.

Too bad she wasn't a cat shifter.

"I'm sorry it took me so long to get my head out of my ass, Sara," Ricky told her, his voice soft. His expression screamed uncertainty as he glanced back and forth between her eyes. "I'd really like to talk to you. Could you shift for me, please?"

Sara didn't want to lose her mate's touch, but he didn't give her any choice. When Ricky released her so he could set the satchel he carried on a nearby log, she knew it was for the best. They really did have a lot to talk about.

Praying to whatever gods cared to listen that Ricky's apology meant he was coming around, Sara began to shift. Her fur receded as did her tail and horns. The muscles and tendons cracked and popped as her body realigned. Within half a minute, Sara's body resumed her human shape, and she slowly rose to her feet.

Ricky sucked in a harsh gasp as he turned from where he'd been spreading the blanket. His lips parted, and his gaze roved over her naked form. His cheeks darkened while a glow of arousal filled his green eyes, causing them to darken.

Sara felt her cheeks heat. So did her neck and breasts as a full body blush blazed through her. As a shifter, she'd stood naked before dozens of men . . . and women . . . but never had anyone stared at her the way Ricky was right that second.

The urge to cover herself stole over Sara, so she did.

Sara's arms moving must have yanked Ricky out of whatever thoughts had been coursing through his mind. He groaned and stepped closer, lifting his hands. After a second of hesitation, he rested them on her upper arms.

"Don't hide from me, honey," Ricky pleaded, his voice husky. "You are so gorgeous you take my breath away."

Then Ricky slid his arms around her as he took the last step between them. He skimmed one hand up to cradle Sara's nape as he dipped his head. Pressing his mouth to hers, Ricky gave Sara her first kiss, sliding his tongue between her slightly parted lips and teasing along her flesh.

Sara gasped as unfamiliar sensations shot through her body. Fire ignited in her veins, and warmth surged southward, pooling at the apex of her thighs. Her stomach fluttered, and her nipples beaded.

Ricky lifted his head and groaned. His eyes appeared to blaze with his lust. He skimmed his thumb along Sara's cheek, causing the hairs on her neck to stand on end in the most delicious of ways.

"I don't know how I resisted you," Ricky whispered, his voice rough. "I don't know why I tried." He rested his forehead against Sara's. "Will you forgive a middle-aged man his foolishness and show me how to love you the way you deserve?"

Swallowing hard, Sara forced herself to admit, "I-I don't know." She cradled Ricky's torso, sliding her thumbs along his t-shirt-hidden ribs. "I've never done anything, Ricky."

After letting out another rough groan, Ricky told her, "Didn't mean that kind of love, but hearing you admit that makes me want you so damn badly." He lifted his head, then swallowed so hard his Adam's apple bobbed. "Meant love as in" — he grimaced — "love . . ." His voice trailed off, and he shook his head, obviously uncertain how to finish.

Sara's heart pounded in her chest as she understood his meaning. Lust, need, and anticipation simmered through her in equal measure. Giving her mate a come hither smile, she wrapped her arms around him as she pushed her lower body against Ricky's own. The hardness she felt pressing against her caused her blood to sing.

Ricky's sharp hiss and the rocking of his hips, how he pushed his erection harder against her, sent Sara's confidence soaring.

Gonna have to thank Jared for that porn account again.

Peering at Ricky through her lashes, Sara whispered, "How about I show you how to love as a couple, and you show me how to make love?"

Groaning once more, Ricky grabbed Sara tight. As he swung her around and lowered her to the blanket, Sara laughed. When Ricky settled over her, Sara spread her legs and welcomed him between her thighs.

"God, yes," Ricky muttered, his gaze roving over her face, neck, and breasts before returning to her face. "Need you so badly."

"And I you, my mate."

Ricky moaned as he rocked against Sara. "Yes," he whispered. "Yes, mate."

When Ricky sealed his mouth over Sara's once again and began driving her out of her ever-loving mind, Sara realized she had finally discovered what she was missing . . . and she was never going to let him go.

CHAPTER ELEVEN

As Jared waited for the others to get into position, he thought about how his life had changed, once again, in the last week. His honorary niece had finally bonded with her man—*thank god*. His home had been destroyed, his biological family thought he was dead, and the corpse his parents had buried had been stolen by Kahlil to be presented to the Sanchez cartel.

At least his family had thought he'd died with his lover. That had given them a small measure of comfort.

And now I'm taking out a known bomb-maker.

What had surprised Jared the most was Beta Dixon's request to come along. And it *had* been a request, too. The beta hadn't demanded. Instead, he'd asked permission from Alpha Declan before making his desire known to Jared.

Jared recalled that conversation.

"You want to fly to Romania to help me capture Castrose Zukan?" When Jared saw Dixon nod, he'd asked the obvious. "Why?"

"A couple of reasons, actually," Dixon had replied, lounging on the love seat across from where Jared and Carson sat. "First, you're pack, and what threatens one person in the pack threatens us all."

Nodding, Jared had lifted one brow. "And the other reason?"

"Everyone speaks very highly of your infiltration skills," Dixon had told him. "I would very much like to see you in action. Plus, it'll give us a chance to get to know each other outside a pack setting."

Jared had narrowed his eyes as he swept his gaze over the huge blond shifter. "Will you be willing to follow my orders?" The request had probably been pushing it, but his need to goad had gotten the better of him.

Dixon had smirked at him. "Any order that won't put my life or anyone else's life in direct danger."

After scoffing, Jared had pointed out, "This mission puts us all in danger."

"Then let's not compound it by asking for anything especially foolish."

Jared had laughed and nodded. "Welcome aboard."

Dixon had been true to his word, too. While the beta had offered ideas, he hadn't insisted on getting his way, acquiescing to Jared's final plan. Dixon had been teamed up with Payson, a hyena shifter with a little too much crazy, but who was fantastic in a fight. That pair was approaching Castrose's place from the north.

Jared, Carson, and Draven were heading in from the south. Kontra, Vail, and Eli—Kontra's python shifter doctor—were heading in from the east. The final team, who was coming in from the west was comprised of Kontra's beta, a Texas longhorn bull shifter named Sam, plus his highly trained mercenary mate, Ryan.

Left at the rendezvous point was Tim, who had cast a spell which allowed him to see through the eyes of a crow shifter named Castor. The avian soared over the forest, searching for anything that could constitute a problem. Guarding Tim's back were a number of others, including two fae who would protect the group with their own brand of magick.

The last small group was led by a lion shifter named Grimes. He guarded the end of an escape tunnel along with Mutegi—a warthog shifter.

"Everyone's in position," Tim commented.

Jared knew that he wasn't alone in starting to creep forward, keeping an eye out for tripwires or other snares.

"Sam, there's a tripwire twenty feet in front of you. Make certain you avoid it."

Sam's grunt came through Jared's earpiece.

"Kontra, a pit begins three steps to your left," Tim advised. "Watch your footing."

"See it. Thanks, love."

"Shit. Dixon freeze," Tim ordered.

"What is it?" Dixon asked. "What do you see."

"A camera in a tree to your right is panning your way," Tim told him. "You and Payson need to ease to your right about twenty feet to get around it."

For the next half hour, that was how it went. Castor swooped around the area, appearing as if he was a crow on the hunt for dinner. Tim would offer words of advice and warnings.

By the time Castrose's house came into view, Jared felt beads of sweat dripping down his back. His muscles were tenser than he could ever remember them. Even his back ached from having to ever-so-carefully bend, crouch, and maneuver through traps . . . and from carrying the duffel with the bomb in it.

"Okay," Tim stated. "All four teams are just in the tree line of the house. Hold position, guys. You're up, Draven."

Draven confirmed, then began to chant. Jared didn't understand the words, but he knew what the vampire was supposed to be doing. Draven had claimed to be able to unlock the front door. He was also supposed to be able to confirm if there were any explosive devices set up anywhere in the house.

"We should be clear," Draven murmured after another ten minutes.

"Should be?" Dixon questioned skeptically.

Drave scoffed. "Magick is not an exact science."

Jared sighed. "I'll do it."

"You most certainly will not," Carson declared.

Resting one hand on Carson's upper arm, Jared used his other to cradle his big lover's jaw. "Injun, the bomb ended up under our SUV. I have to do this."

"No," Carson countered again, taking the bag and slinging the strap over his own shoulder. Before Jared could try another way to convince him, his lover teased the backs of his forefingers over his jaw and told him, "*Our* SUV, remember? *We* have to do this."

Jared's chest tightened at the idea of Carson being in the line of fire if the door was booby-trapped in a way that Draven couldn't divine. Then he remembered that Carson would be feeling the exact same way if it were reversed. After an internal groan, Jared nodded.

"Okay."

"Good luck, gentlemen," Kontra rumbled through their com line.

Fighting back his urge to roll his eyes, Jared softly replied, "Thanks." He slid his hand into Carson's and twined their fingers.

Together, they stepped out of the safety of the tree cover.

Jared refused to show weakness and forced his legs to continue moving. One foot in front of the other, he made his way to the front door of Castrose Zukan's retreat. The place appeared to be a ramshackle cottage tucked deep in the woods. The siding was faded, a few shingles were missing from the roof, and even the paint on the shutters was peeling.

All in all, the place looked deserted.

Jared hoped that appearances were deceiving.

Once he'd reached the stoop, Jared gripped the doorknob.

After a second, he turned it. When nothing happened, Jared let out a breath he hadn't even realized he'd been holding.

Damn!

After exchanging a look with his lover, Jared pushed the door open and headed into the house. He felt his heart sink to his feet when he saw the state of the interior. Dust covered the scuffed hardwood floors, marred only by critter tracks and mouse turds. There was no furniture in the front room.

Not giving up, Jared crept forward. Carson was at his side. Together, they began clearing each room.

Jared was beginning to wonder if they'd struck out when an odd pattern in the dirt on the floor of what was probably the kitchen caught his attention. There were just the faintest line marks in a swirling pattern. It almost appeared as if someone had attempted to smooth out the dust.

Crouching beside it, Jared took a closer look. He placed his fingertips through it and slid them along the streaks. Then he grinned up at his mate.

"Scratches are hidden under here," Jared told Carson. "Let's see if we can find out what caused them."

They both began searching the nearby walls for any sign of a hidden door. Carson growled his pleasure when a section of the floor suddenly swung upward. Jared had to make a quick step left to keep from sliding onto his ass.

Jared nodded, pleasure filling him as he peered down the stairs into the darkness. "Nice, Injun." He swept his gaze over the kitchen again. "Where was the switch?"

Carson pointed out a small knothole in the wall almost hidden behind a three-legged table. The fourth leg had been broken off, and it leaned against the wall. Just the slightest marring on that wall showed where it had repeatedly been jostled by someone coming and going.

"Think he's down there? Or out?" Then Carson shook his head as he indicated the floor. "If he was in there, wouldn't the dust have been stacked against the wall like it is now?"

Jared mentally agreed even as he mulled over the question. Something else caught his attention. "What's this?" He leaned over to inspect the cupboard door that ran right along the trap door. Sliding his finger into a groove in the wood, Jared tugged, and the panel easily opened.

Along with the door came a metal arm attached to it at one end. On the other end was a broom. As the door opened and swung shut, the broom came out and swept the floor right where the door would have been if closed.

"Holy shit," Carson stated. "So he can cover his tracks if he's inside."

Grinning broadly, Jared indicated the stairway down. "Shall we go?"

"I hate walking into the unknown."

Jared nodded. "So do I."

"Then let us help," Kontra stated through the line, reminding Jared that everyone could hear every word they said. "That's what we're here for."

"Okay," Jared replied. "Once we reach the bottom of the stairs, if nothing happens, come on down. The trap door is in the kitchen."

After receiving an acknowledgement from Kontra and the others, Jared headed down the stairs. He felt the heat of his lover at his back and knew Carson stayed close. The sensation was reassuring in a way and set his heart racing as well.

Jared reached the bottom and glanced around. The tunnel before him was lined with rock and stretched almost fifty feet. There were no tunnels or doors, but he spotted a glow in the distance.

"Only one way to go," Carson whispered into his ear.

Nodding, Jared started forward. At the end of the hallway, there was a sharp curve to the left. Ever-so-carefully, he dipped his head around the corner, then pulled it back. Jared tried to process what he'd seen, but it didn't make sense.

Jared took in a deep breath, pulled his gun from his holster, and rounded the corner. Slowly, he made his way into the massive room. He spotted a bed in the back to the left and a shower stall, toilet, and sink to the right. There was a kitchen in the closer left corner and a small two-seater table halfway between the kitchen and the bed. In the front right corner was a massive electronics system with half a dozen monitors hanging on the wall over a desk.

The middle of the room was dominated by a massive table. Under the table were a plethora of plastic storage bins. Some had two drawers, and some had three.

A man sat at the table, and when he lifted his head, he didn't seem in the slightest bit surprised by Jared's arrival.

The man had magnifying glasses covering his eyes, and when he lifted his head and peered at Jared, he smiled. "I have never seen anyone get even close to what you and your team did," he commented as he continued to glance down at whatever he was working on. "Please. Sit." He waved at a rolling stool that was resting before his electronics. "Bring that over. Just give me two minutes to finish this fuse. Wouldn't want this to blow up in our faces, eh?"

Jared glanced back at Carson, but his lover appeared just as confused as he felt. As he crossed to the rolling stool, Jared ordered, "Give us a minute, Kontra. I-I'm not sure if this is Castrose or not." The man before him looked *nothing* like the picture he'd seen of Castrose Zukan.

The military photo of Castrose was a tall, blond man with a military-fit body weighing in at two hundred twenty pounds. His dossier indicated he stood six-foot-four, and he was a specialist in hand-to-hand combat. His superiors had stated he was a cold, unfriendly loaner.

The man at the table, while blond, was none of the other things. If Jared had to guess, the guy was maybe a buck-thirty. Even while sitting, he knew the little fellow couldn't stand more than five-foot-seven.

After rolling the stool over, Jared sat. He waited patiently. When he heard the man give a soft grunt of pleasure, he realized the guy had finished whatever he'd been soldering.

The man put down the soldering iron and lifted his magnifying safety glasses. He slid the device he was working on toward the center of the table, then folded his hands before him. Leaning on his forearms, he grinned.

"So. How did you get through the traps?"

"Are you Castrose Zukan?" Carson asked bluntly.

Shrugging, the man snickered. "You wouldn't be here if I wasn't who you were looking for." Castrose waggled his brows as he swept his gaze up and down their bodies. "Not what you expected, right?" He winked one blue eye as he leered at them. "You're not what I expected, either. Definitely not military. You didn't use a drone to avoid the traps, and there's no one I know that could have disabled the explosive attached to the front door." Cocking his head, Castrose continued to smile. "So. Who are you?"

Jared couldn't figure out how to respond. All his brain was saying was . . . *what the fuck*?

CHAPTER TWELVE

Carson knew Jared was reeling. This small man wasn't what they'd expected at all. Still, they needed answers . . . and the man seemed just eccentric enough to be a straight shooter.

"How about you answer our questions, and we'll answer yours?" Carson lifted the bag he'd been carrying and placed it on the table. "I'll even start. Deal?"

Castrose lifted one blond brow as he eyed the bag, but he nodded anyway. "All right." He unfolded a hand, waving in a *go ahead* motion. "So, not military or with a government?"

Carson shook his head. "We are not military. We are not working with a government. We tracked you down for a private matter." Keeping the duffel bag closed, he decided to ask, "How come you don't match your military file?"

Snorting, Castrose rolled his eyes. "I've never been in the military. That was my brother. I'm Clayton."

That was when it hit Carson. The man hadn't actually confirmed his name when he'd asked earlier. "So . . . your brother is Castrose, and you are Clayton?"

"Yup." Then Clayton pointed between them. "So, you and your team. There's a lot of you, but you're not military. You're not with a government." He frowned. "How did you get through all of Castrose's booby traps? He's damn good at them." Clayton waved his hand at the device he was working on as well as the tools littering the table. "Just like I'm amazing at bombs."

Carson cocked his head, wondering about the best way to

answer that. He needed Clayton's continued cooperation. Except, for the truth, he needed permission.

"Dixon?"

"Listening," the beta replied.

"Permission to be truthful with Clayton?" Carson spotted the way Clayton's brows rose, so just held the man's gaze as he smiled.

A low rumble came through the line. "You should warn him that if he wants that answer, he will be coming with us."

Carson relayed that information.

Cocking his head, Clayton gave him a narrow-eyed stare. "And why would I do that?"

"Because just as you value your secrecy" — Carson swept his hand around the space, then pointed upstairs — "our secrecy is just as important. Without it, neither of us would continue with our current existence."

Clayton crossed his arms over his chest and leaned back in his chair. "Where would I be taken?"

"A place called Stone Ridge, Colorado."

"Do you have a problem with gays?"

Barking a laugh, Carson cradled Jared's jaw. He urged his lover to tip his head back while bending at the waist. Sealing his mouth over his mate's, he gave him a thorough tongue-fucking, delving deep and tasting his man, loving every second of it.

"Guess not," Clayton mumbled breathily.

Figuring he'd put on enough of a show, Carson broke the kiss. Except, he couldn't resist pecking at Jared's lips one more time. Then he lifted his head and smirked at Clayton.

Humming, Clayton murmured, "Got a brother?"

Carson laughed. "I do not. But I have friends who swing your way."

"Nice. So" — Clayton waved between them — "what's your story? What are you doing here?" He crossed his arms over his chest as he narrowed his eyes. "And I still want to know how you got past my brother's traps."

"First, we're here to ask who you sold this to." Carson finally opened the bag, buying himself time to think. Explaining paranormals was never easy. Shoving down the sides of the black duffel bag, Carson revealed the bomb. "Recognize this?"

Clayton leaped to his feet as a gasp escaped him. Grabbing the bag strap, he pulled it close. "Oh my god," he whispered, poking at wiring here and there. "What did you do to it?" Then Clayton scowled at them. "And how did you get it?"

"What we did to it is called disarming it, so we weren't blown to bits," Jared replied, evidently finally finding his voice. "And I took it with me so I could track you."

Perhaps hearing the lethal anger in Jared's voice, Clayton straightened where he stood staring at his bomb. "And you are?"

"Jared Templeton." He held out his hand. "A pleasure to make your acquaintance."

"You're the guy who assassinated Larson's big brother," Clayton murmured softly even as he took Jared's hand and shook it. "And I've heard about some of your other hits." Then his brows furrowed as he released Jared's hand. "Although, now that I think about it, other than taking out Larson's brother, I haven't heard of you doing anything in a while . . . and it was under the name Coleson."

"So you sold Larson a bomb because he claimed Jared killed his brother?" Carson seriously wanted to wring the damn wolf's neck. "And it wasn't true, by the way."

"Or do you just sell them to whoever?" Jared mused, his tone beyond dry to challenging. "As long as they have the money, they can buy a bomb?"

To Carson's shock, Clayton gaped, his eyes widening. He

looked . . . offended. His words confirmed it.

"I'll have you know that I always check to see where my bombs are going," Clayton stated, crossing his arms over his chest. "He had evidence that you took out his brother."

Jared smirked at Carson. "I didn't even know Larson had a brother."

"Certainly didn't mention it to me, but at least we know it wasn't some other asshole who set it." Carson rested his hand on Jared's nape and squeezed rhythmically. "Only problem is, we still don't know how many people he told about you."

Shrugging, Jared told him, "It doesn't matter. I'm already dead, remember? And the pack is keeping an eye on my relatives until things settle down." He rose to his feet. "In the meantime, we'll keep watching the organizations Kahlil told us about, and Raul can keep tracking down Larson's hairy ass."

"Wait, where are you going?" Clayton demanded. "You can't leave until you tell me how you got past my traps."

Carson had to admit that the little fellow had balls. "Well, you see, we're paranormals. Faster reflexes. Stronger. Tougher." Shrugging, he added, "Plus, we did have a drone of a sort monitoring things."

Scoffing, Clayton shook his head. "I would have spotted a drone."

"Did you notice the huge crow circling the area?" Jared asked, smirking. "*He* was our drone, and the warlock connected with him was our eyes."

Clayton snickered as he rolled his eyes. "Seriously?" He grinned as he glanced between them. "You're really gonna try to feed me a line about super creatures and magick?"

"Since you're coming with us, you'll see soon enough for yourself," Carson stated. "We—"

"There's a whole lot of military slipping into the area,"

Tim stated, tension bleeding through the line. "Looks like someone tipped off Castrose's location. Looks like Romanian. You all need to get out of there."

"Shit," Jared hissed. Turning to Clayton, he ordered, "Pack what you need. It's time to go."

"Why?" Clayton took a step backward.

"Because the Romanian military is on its way to storm your compound," Jared told him. "And I don't think they're going to be nearly as understanding as I am."

Clayton's eyes widened, and he shook his head. "I can't leave now. I have to wait for Castrose. He's going to be back tomorrow. He—"

"They're twenty minutes out," Tim told them.

"You'll have to leave him a message on his phone or something," Carson told him gruffly. "Where's the entrance to your escape tunnel? We have to use it. Now!"

Instead of answering them, Clayton rushed over to his electronics. A touch of a button had his monitors flaring to life. "Shit," he whispered as he took in the myriad of men in black easing through the forest toward his house.

Then Clayton began rushing around the room.

"The tunnel, Clayton?" Carson demanded as he watched Jared begin fiddling with something on the bomb in the bag. "Where?"

Clayton pointed toward the shower. "Turn the showerhead clockwise a quarter turn, then pull the hot knob." Then he returned to tossing certain things into a couple of bags.

Carson did as he was told. A second later, the entire shower assembly shifted five feet to the right. Peering into the five-foot wide, six-foot tall tunnel that appeared, Carson pulled a flashlight from his belt and clicked it on.

Cobwebs stretched across the space, but Carson knew spiders were the least of their worries.

"Are you ready?" Carson asked as he turned his attention

back to the monitors. He noticed those with him seemed to all but melt into the woods. The soldiers completely missed them as they made their way toward the house.

"Yeah," Clayton replied, his nerves making his voice waver. "Y-You really aren't going to turn me over to them?"

Carson swept his gaze over the man, seeing that he had a backpack slung over his shoulder, carried a second in his left hand, and held a pistol in his other one. Pointing at it, he asked, "Since you weren't in the military, I have to ask if you know how to use that." Carson watched as Clayton's expression turned offended, so he lifted a hand in placation. "I have no desire to be shot in the back if you trip."

Clayton huffed in annoyance. "I taught Castrose everything he ever learned about bombs, and he taught me to use a gun." Carson must have given away his disbelief, for Clayton snapped, "He was in the military. A big, buff soldier. Who would pay our prices if they knew it was some no-name geek making them?"

"He's right," Jared stated, coming up behind them. "It's time to go."

Carson noticed only the flashlight in Jared's hand, so he looked beyond him to the duffel bag on the table. "We're leaving that?"

Jared grinned and waggled his eyebrows. "Yep. Can't have anyone discovering my fingerprints on anything. I'm dead, remember?"

Realizing what Jared was telling him, Carson grumbled, "Oh for the love of—" He didn't bother finishing. Instead, he hustled into the tunnel.

As soon as all three of them were in the tunnel, everything grew darker.

Carson glanced over his shoulder and noticed that the door had been closed behind them. "We're in the tunnel. Coming to you, Grimes."

"We're waiting," the big lion shifter replied.

"Shit! You had people waiting at the exit of my tunnel?" Clayton all but squeaked.

Jared chuckled. "Of course."

"You're thorough," Clayton grumbled. "How'd you even know about it?"

"Because I was looking for it," Jared told him. "It's how I escaped my own home, so I knew you probably had one, too."

The trio fell into silence as they hustled down the tunnel. When they reached the end, Carson nearly ran face-first into the door. He'd had his head turned, so he could look over his shoulder and check the other men's progress.

"Damn," Carson grumbled, rubbing his forearm as he searched for the doorknob.

"What's wrong?" Kontra immediately asked. "What's going on?"

"Just a scratch in the tunnel," Carson told the other shifter. "Everything's fine. We're at the exit."

Before Kontra could respond, a deep rumbling shudder rolled through the ground. At the same time, a massive boom sounded from behind them. Then a harsh whooshing sound filled Carson's ears.

"Mooove!" Jared yelled.

Carson obeyed, turning the knob. His mate shoved both of them through the open doorway. While Grimes grabbed Clayton, who squeaked in alarm, Jared pushed Carson to the right and onto the ground.

The roaring grew louder, and suddenly a burst of flame shot through the tunnel opening behind them. It singed Carson's hair and caused the soles of his shoes to melt. When it eventually subsided, he could finally take in a deep breath.

Twisting around, Carson shoved Jared off of him. He immediately began checking his mate for injuries. After patting out a couple of smoldering embers on the legs of Jared's jeans, he checked him over again.

"Are you okay?" Carson asked, fear adding a sense of urgency to his voice.

"Damn it," Jared grumbled. "I thought the tunnel was shorter."

Carson huffed a sigh, then captured his lover's lips. Thrusting his tongue into the man's mouth, he lapped and teased at him. He relished the feel of Jared's tongue sliding against his own, kissing him back.

At the same time, Carson began sliding his hands all over Jared's body. He pushed under his shirt, scraping over his flesh and searching for injuries. When breathing became a need instead of a want, Carson finally broke the kiss. He scowled down at his lover.

"Don't fucking do that ever again," Carson demanded.

Jared hummed as he threaded his fingers through Carson's hair. "Wasn't on purpose, Injun." His expression grew serious. "Are you injured, love?"

Carson dipped his head and pressed another slow, lingering, sipping kiss to his Jared's lips. "No, my mate."

"Well, if you're not injured, could you get up, please?" Grimes stated gruffly. "We need to get out of here."

Groaning, Carson nodded. He forced himself to release his lover and push to his feet. When he offered his hand, Jared took it, and Carson pulled him up and into his arms, tucking him close.

"So, do you have a place where we can keep talking to our new friend here?" Grimes asked curiously as he guided a pensive-looking Clayton through the woods.

"Naw, man," Jared replied glibly. "Take him to Dixon. That'll all be on him."

Carson nearly missed a step. "You don't want to question him?"

Jared shook his head. "No, our beta can handle it."

"Such a vote of confidence," Dixon said through the com line. "Still, I'm curious as to why you'd give up the privilege."

Laughing, Jared pinned a feral grin on Carson. "Because as of right now, I'm on vacation."

Carson moaned before dipping his head and kissing him. He was all on board for that idea. As Carson explored Jared's mouth, reveling in how amazing his mate tasted and felt in his arms, only one thought flitted through his mind.

Me, Jared, and a private, sandy beach. That'll be about damn perfect.

You may also enjoy the following from eXtasy Books Inc:

Burning the Chef's Buns
Charlie Richards

Excerpt

"The last of the perimeter cameras have been installed," Seever Kerns told his best friend and boss, Councilman Vincentius Goldstein. Leaning against the closed door behind him, he crossed his arms over his chest as he grinned broadly. "I told you I could get it done in three days."

Vincentius chuckled as he lifted his hands in surrender. "You were right." Then his smile turned wry as he swept his gaze over him. "You look like shit, though. Go to bed."

Seever would have laughed, but he was too busy fighting back a yawn. His fellow lion shifter was right. He was damn exhausted, hardly able to stay on his feet. Still, the extra effort was worth it.

I made the damn place safer for the little fliers.

Several months before, Vincentius's systems had been hacked, prompting the councilman to order the hacker tracked down and brought to the estate for questioning. It had been discovered that the man had been a guinea fowl shifter named Cho . . . and he'd turned out to be Vincentius's mate. Seever guessed he'd had to do a bit of groveling at some point, since the little man had forgiven him, and they'd bonded.

Cho wasn't the only one they'd added to their household that day, though. A few days later, the shifter's whole flock and their mates — or those who had them — had arrived. That had been nearly another dozen people.

Good thing this estate is massive.

Many of the new arrivals brought out the protective instincts of the people in security — Seever included. As the head of the household's security, the safety of everyone was his primary concern. Sadly, with the escape of a couple of ex-councilmen and several enforcers going rogue with them, his job had become even more difficult.

Shaking his head, Vincentius offered him a bemused smile. "I really am grateful for everything you do for me, See. Thank you."

"I'm on my way to bed soon. Shower first, though," Seever told Vincentius, pushing off the door. "And you never have to thank me. This is our home and our family."

"I'm glad to hear you say that." Vincentius's brows furrowed as he peered up at him from where he sat. "I occasionally worry, since we both know your lion is quite a bit more dominant than mine, but to outward appearances, you answer to me."

Seever snorted, his lips curving into a wry smirk. "What other people think is irrelevant," he stated, resting his hand on the doorknob. While he really wanted to get out of there so he could enjoy that shower he'd mentioned, he wouldn't walk away from his friend in the middle of the conversation. "We have a system that works, and that's between us."

Vincentius nodded. "I'll start incorporating the cameras into the system right now then."

The abrupt subject change didn't concern Seever. He and the councilman didn't make a habit of sharing their feelings. On occasion, they would talk about their problems over a drink, but that had been before Vincentius had bonded with Cho.

Now I get to shoot the shit with almost a dozen guys as I avoid Prescott's come-ons.

Seever mentally laughed at his thought as he twisted the knob and opened the office door. Gods, I must be tired. Smirking, he began exiting the room.

"Oh, hey, Seever," Vincentius called, causing Seever to turn back around. "This afternoon, I heard from Rocky that his cousin is visiting next week."

"His cousin?" Pausing tiredly, Seever rested his forearm on the doorframe. He leaned his temple on it as he eyed his boss, forcing his sluggish brain to focus. "Okay. Uh . . . I'm assuming Rocky gave you his name and shit, so you could run a background check? Get a picture?"

As the head of security to the estate of a man on the Shifter Council, he liked to know who would be wandering around the area. Knowing a person beforehand often headed off problems before they might arise. Plus, if some random dude appeared at the gate that they weren't expecting, it was Seever's job to verify who they were and if it was safe to allow them on the property.

Vincentius obviously recognized Seever's fatigue, for he concisely stated, "Yeah, Rocky said his name is Reese Nelson. I'll forward his picture and information to you." His eyes narrowed as he warned, "Do not start it now. Go get your shower and pass out."

Nodding, Seever silently agreed. "No way I could stay awake right now anyway." Even though he hated to admit to weakness, even to his buddy, he had to share the truth. Pulling his phone off the clip at his belt, Seever checked the time. A little after two in the afternoon. "I can't imagine that I'm gonna wake again today. I'll look at it in the morning."

Giving Seever a thumbs up, Vincentius stated, "The info will be in your inbox when you wake." Then he gave Seever a knowing look as he added, "And I won't be sending it for at least an hour, so you won't be tempted."

Seever scoffed. "You know me too well."

With a wave of his hand, Vincentius turned back to his computer systems.

Closing the door, Seever headed down the hall and stopped at a door a short way from the councilman's computer room. He occupied an apartment-like suite on the front side of the home. His boss's—and recently Cho's—set of rooms were on the other side of the hall facing the gorgeous rear expanse of lawns. People who also occupied the other sets of rooms in their wing were Alpha Ashton—the leader of Cho's flock—and his mate, Ranger. Then across from them on the backside was his beta, Gilbert, and his mate, Hess.

The upper floor of the estate's opposite wing that had once been reserved for guests, even though it was rarely used, was now occupied by the rest of the flock and their mates. The lower floors were home to guards and staff as well as a nicely equipped security suite.

Dismissing everything, Seever gave in to his body's needs. He stopped in his closet and stripped his jeans and t-shirt. Once nude, he headed to his ensuite and turned on his shower.

One of the nice perks of living in a fancy estate was fantastic water pressure and several high-end waterfall shower heads. Resting his forearms on the tile, he laid his forehead on his right one.

Seever groaned deeply as he reveled in the hot spray pounding on his exhausted muscles. He'd been awake for nearly forty hours, and his body was telling him he'd overdone it. Still, Seever had needed all those cameras and motion detectors up.

Now, even if a mouse shifter came onto the property while in animal form, their security team would know about it. Of course, that also meant they would be checking out a lot more wildlife, too. Shifters came in all shapes and sizes—

from spider to elephant — so their security people were going to become really good at tracking the natural hunting paths of their huge estate's normal animals.

Sadly, that meant being aware that someone could be watching if someone decided to have sex out in the woods.

That thought caused Seever to smile as his thoughts drifted once again to Prescott. The man was a very sensuous wood duck shifter. He had a lean, lithe build, and his pale blue eyes always held a wealth of flirtatiousness.

Seever had never fucked where he lived before, but with Prescott's constant advances and innuendo, he was damn tempted to change that.

Thinking about the pretty man, Seever felt his prick plump a little. Too bad he was too tired to even jack off. Shaking his head, he grabbed his body wash and loofah and got to work cleaning himself.

Don't want to pass out in the shower.

Once Seever had finished scrubbing off nearly two days of sweat, he shut off the water and exited the huge space. He grabbed the towel and began rubbing himself dry even as he left the bathroom. His eyelids slipped closed as his damp feet sank into the lush carpet of his bedroom.

Pausing, Seever swayed as he rubbed over himself. He let out a deep sigh and tipped his head down, then snapped his eyelids back open. Shaking his head, he dropped the towel on the floor and crossed the last couple of steps to the bed.

Seever flopped face-first onto his bed, using the last of his strength to swing his legs onto the mattress. He groaned and stretched before finally succumbing to his body's need for rest.

About the Author

Charlie started writing fantasy when she was eight, and after stumbling onto her first erotic romance at age nineteen, she realized her true calling. She now focuses on writing gay erotic romance, normally of the paranormal variety, with heroes of all kinds. With the help and support of her husband, Charlie finally fulfilled one of her life-long goals . . . move to acreage with her horses. You can often find her curled up with her laptop and a cup of tea or glass of wine, creating her next adventure. Charlie enjoys exploring the mountains of her new Oregon home on horseback, 4-wheeler, or motorcycle.

She can be reached at ch.richards2010@yahoo.com or visit her at www.charlie-richards.com